Murat Tuncel

Wilma's Treasure Trunk

Short Stories

Translated by Stuart Kline

Edited by Richard Holmes

Wilma's Treasure Trunk
Short Stories

©2023 Murat Tuncel
ISBN: 978-3-910667-00-6

Translated from the Turkish
by Stuart Kline
Edited by Richard Holmes

Published by
Texianer Verlag
Tuningen
Germany
www.texianer.com

Contents

About the Author Murat Tuncel...5
Foreword..9
Zaida the Flower Girl..11
Kidnapping in The Hague...23
Doves..39
Wilma's Treasure Trunk..49
Roberto Bienco...61
Honor...71
Switchblade Time...83
Snowy Images...99
The Girl with the Silver Voice..107
The Fish and The Monument...117
Funeral Preludes...125
Refugees...137
Aristotle..193

About the Author
Murat Tuncel

Born in 1952 in the town of Hanak in Turkey's eastern province of Kars, Tuncel graduated from primary and secondary school, then graduated from Teachers' School in Artvin province. He then graduated from the Turkish Department of Istanbul Atatürk Faculty of Education in 1979. He subsequently was employed at primary and secondary schools throughout the country. Tuncel quit teaching and began working for *Günaydın* newspaper in 1984. Five years later, he left Turkey to live in the Netherlands. Continuing his literary career in the Netherlands, the author gave native language lessons at a basic education school affiliated with the Dutch Ministry of Education as well as Turkish language and literature lessons at the Rotterdam Conservatory.

While the author's first story was published in 1981, his stories and articles were subsequently published in Turkish literary magazines such as *Varlık, Edebiyat Gündemi, Damar, Yaşasın Edebiyat, Kıyı, Karşı Edebiyat, Turneç, Türk Dili Dergisi, Güzel Yazılar, Evrensel Kültür, Folklor Edebiyat, Ürün, Sincan İstasyonu,* and *Edebiyat Gündemi.* In having his stories and articles published in many magazines and anthologies in the Netherlands where he lived, the author had his novel Maviydi Adalet Sarayı published in Dutch under the name of *Valse Hoop* (False Hope). Moreover, many of the author's stories have since appeared in Dutch, Polish and Russian anthologies. His book of stories called *Gölge Kız* (Shadow Girl) was published in German and Russian.

Subsequent to the author's novel *Üçüncü Ölüm (The Third Death)*, which was published in English, *Inanna* was also published in English, Arabic, Korean and Bulgarian by various publishing houses. The author is a member of the Turkish Writers' Union, the Netherlands Writers' Union, the Turkish Journalists' Association, the Turkish PEN Club and the Literary Union.

Awards

Tuncel was awarded the Youth Story Award, organized jointly by the Ministry of Culture and Sports for his short story *Çerçi* in 1979, 1997 NPS Radio Short Story Award for his short story *Cennet de Bitti (Heaven's Over As Well)*,1994 Şükrü Gümüş Novel Award for his novel *Maviydi Adalet Sarayı* (The Palace of Justice was blue), as well as the 1997 Orhan Kemal Short Story Award for his short story *Gölge Kız(Shadow Girl)*, and the novel *Üçüncü Ölüm* (The Third Death) 1997 Community Centers Culture-Art Competition Novel Award.

Works

Short Stories

Dargın Değilim Yaşama (*I'm Not Offended to Live*, 1981), *Mengelez* (1983), *Güneşsiz Dünya* (*Sunless World*-1987), *Beyoğlu Çığlıkları* (Cries of Beyoğlu *1989), Gölge Kız (Shadow Girl-2002,2004, 2010, 2018) and Wilma'nın Sandığı (Wilma's Treasure Trunk-2010, 2014).*

Children's stories and children's novels

Tipi (Snowstorm- *Esin end Ceylan Publishing* 1982, 2000), *Buluta Binen Uçak (Airplane Riding in the Cloud-Esin Publishing 1983), Tullu Kurbağa* (Super Frog- novel-*Esin Publications 1984 Istanbul, Ortadoğu Ferlag-Germany 1996, Engin Publications 2000, Morpa Publications 2004 Istanbul), Ressamlar Mahallesi'nin Çocukları (Children of the Painters District-2014-2018-Morpa Yayınları, Şakacı Masallar (Morpa Publications-2006/2016).*

Novels

Maviydi Adalet Sarayı (The Palace of Justice was blue), which gives cutaways from the lives of our people living in the Netherlands (Pencere 1994, two editions in Dutch

Uitgeverıj 3C 2003-2004 as *Valse Hoop*, Arnhem) and *Liscus Uitgevrij* 2007 as audiobook CD, Altın Bilek Publications 2007, Istanbul. *Üçüncü Ölüm (The Third Death)*, which is about the life of a Hungarian (People's Publications 1997, Pencere Publications 1998, Altın Bilek Publications 2007), Inanna (Varlık Publications, 2006, 2010, Elfene Dünya Publicasions 2018).

Memoirs:

Yarımağız Anılar (1996 Pencere).

Information about the author:

Dictionary of Who's Who in our Literature (Behçet Necatigil-Varlık),
Encyclopedia of Writers from the Tanzimat to the Present (YKY),
Writers' Anthology (Ihsan Işık-Ankara),
Journalists Association of Turkey Almanacs. (Istanbul),
www.google.com/www.edebiyat.nl

Foreword

Every life is a theatrical play and has its own intriguing story. But there are some lives that don't dovetail into plays or stories. Their lives exceeded the dimensions of one particular story or play, transforming into a chain of stories and plays.

While I was constructing the story of their strange life, I found myself on stage in a play. Nobody told me to act in it. I'm a volunteer actor in this play.

The theater is where this play, in which I'm an actor, opens its curtains while you're snoozing away in your warm, comfy bed. Sometimes after a one-act play is played, it closes its curtains before midnight, and sometimes it stays open until the morning to watch the awakening of those in the bosom of sleep. I'm the one who plays in and watches this strange game until the stories are yours.

When the stories are yours, my acting as well as my spectatorship is over. The curtain of your theater goes up the moment my acting as well as my spectatorship end. Then maybe I'll fall into a deep slumber. Then again, maybe I'll fall into the trap of a new story and forget about sleep.

Those who lived before us said, "Actually, there are no other stories." But when I listened to the stories of my characters whose stories I wrote, I decided that what was said was not true and believed that the story of every moment was different. But there's neither a moment nor time in their story. They divided time in their stories, which they lived like a play. So I blended the time they had disintegrated and put it back into the stories.

You'll seek the parts in that blended time. Maybe most of you will be unable to find those pieces and you won't be able to come to a conclusion all at once. That's because their story has both divided time and turned it into a series of intertwined times. More precisely, the story of their lives has become a story within a play, a play within a story. It's up to you to both read and act.

As you'll see, you'll become an actor in your own way in these stories. Ok, I was with you this far. After this, we go our separate ways. You're not obliged to come to the same conclusions I reached. You read the stories I wrote, but you can both come to the conclusion of your own story and act your own stories on stage…

Zaida the Flower Girl

Hearing what sounded like the soft moaning of the wind, the tremor he had forgotten years ago swept through his body again. He threw his quilt off in fear. He grimaced, as if regretting what she had done as she watched the quilt slip to the floor. As his anxious gaze wandered across the walls painted a pale blue, he noticed that his back and forehead were sweating. He reached out and took the towel he had placed under her pillow before going to bed. As he tried wiping the sweat from his brow, he felt a quiver from his muscles to his viscera and shuffle his internal organs into his stomach. Realizing he didn't have time to think or to wipe his brow, he dashed off to the sink. He bent down and leaned his chest against the edge of the sink. He retched a few times. When nothing came out of his retching, the cold water from the tap he opened hit his face with both hands. He blinked open his eyes, which were shut as the water splashed. He picked up the small towel hanging from a hook on the dirty yellow wall. Wiping her face with the towel, she saw herself in the mirror. The towel in her hand looked like it was stuck to her cheek. He was nervous that the towel was sticking to her face like that, and he immediately moved the towel away from her cheek. "She liked green," he said as he stared into her face and eyes. He was startled when these three words, which he had long forgotten, suddenly came to mind. As his words grew heavier, he feared being crushed under them. He quickly lowered his head and started splashing cold water on his face with both hands again. His hands didn't stop until she was out of breath. As he swept back and forth through his complex emotions, he touched her face with one hand while holding the other hand under the even colder water. "She liked green very much," he said, slowly lifting his head and looking into the mirror again. The words "very much" again weighed heavily upon his heart. He flinched at the touch of the tips of his fingers touching her cheek. He swapped his hands. The cool fingertips of his wet hand, which he held under the cold water, cooled both his skin and his mind a little, but this situation passed shortly and his uneasiness increased.

He was surprised the fingers touching her cheek were his own. "Her sound was green anyway," he said, looking at his fingers. He had turned towards the shower as if he had fled from his white face in the mirror, but he was swelled up again. He hurriedly turned around and pressed his head beneath the gurgling cold water from the faucet. He stayed that way until his scalp, covered by his thick hair, got cold. When the swelling in his stomach completely disappeared, he lifted his head. The water running down his hair got his pajamas all wet. He reached out and picked up the large dark green towel hanging on the other side of the mirror. He gently placed it on top of his hair. After waiting a bit, he began to dry his hair as if he was tearing it out. The movement of his arms slowed once his scalp began hurting. While calmly drying his hair, he averted his glance from the mirror so as not to look at his face. When he was done, he hung up the green towel. As he closed the door, he shook his head and said, "Nope." Grabbing the wet collar of his pajamas, he emerged from the bathroom. With slow steps, he proceeded to the double bed right next to the single bed he slept on. He stopped and looked broadly at the bed. Turning towards the wall, he realized that the door to the wardrobe in the room wasn't there.

While looking at the wardrobe, he muttered, "Was it like that yesterday?" He looked at the triple bed again. "I wonder if she ever came and stayed here again?" he asked. Sitting on the single bed, he saw her face buried in darkness on the polished sideboard of the doorless closet. He looked at himself as if he had seen someone else. Trying not to look at himself, he grabbed the quilt that he had just thrown off of his side of the bed, and spread it on top the mattress with two hands. "This quilt is as green as her face," he said as he straightened the quilt. Smiling as if an imp had awakened inside her, he leapt onto the double bed next to him. Suddenly, he started jumping on the bed with all the childish enthusiasm in the world. When he got tired, he lay on his back, sprawled out as if he were going to fill the huge bed. All enthusiasm faded as his gaze began to roam the ceiling from where he was lying. He semi-straightened up. He picked up three pillows from one side of the bed to support his back. He leaned back against the pillows and looked at the wide glass window from wall to wall. He got up and opened the thick velvet curtains. He went and leaned back against the pillows again and gazed out at Dampoort Square from the wall-to-wall window of his room. The wide window seemed to embrace the square. From the window, he could easily see the bus stops in the square, the parked cars, the roads around the square, the small signs hung on concrete posts on both sides of the roads, contradicting everything. At one point, he had the impression that all the people waiting for the bus, lined up at the bus stops, were looking at him. He peered at those standing in line. No one cared or even looked at her. He was relieved.

But while he continued staring, he muttered in bewilderment, "Never mind looking at me, they're not even looking at each other."

From the wide bridge just ahead of the square came a noise that sounded like a snake rubbing against dried leaves on hot sand. The noise quickly increased in volume, drowning out all the sounds around, when a passenger train with colorful wagons, running with the haste of lambs fleeing a heatwave, clacked its way over the bridge. It seemed to him the train was travelling southbound, but he couldn't quite tell which side was north and which side was south. While looking at the colorful wagons that seemed as though they were racing to pass each other behind the locomotive, he muttered, "it's as if a car's been added in every country it passes."

Moving away as if its eyes were searching or chasing something, the train had just disappeared when another train came into sight from the opposite direction. "Let her go northbound," he said, smiling.

This time his gaze moved afar as the carriages of the second train went off into the distance. He was getting ready to send her gaze further away in his mind when yet a third train came into the frame. It wasn't like the previous two trains, in that it didn't make the hissing sound of a locomotive. When it disappeared in a hurry, as if to catch up to the first train, an articulated bus, which seemed to be waiting for it to leave, also departed the stop in the square. The railroad was silent as if it was resting, but this time, cars filled the street beneath the railroad overpass. For a moment, there was no sound except buses moving one after another from the stops in the square and vehicles passing under the overpass. An unbearable silence enveloped the place as both cars and buses swept along the roads around the square to reach their destinations. He was just as afraid of the silence as she was afraid of her trembling just now. He looked at everything in the room as if seeing it for the first time. As he hurried off the double bed, muttering, "The walls were painted green when we arrived." He ripped off his pajamas, put on his pants, shirt, socks, shoes, and took his jacket and exited the room. He turned the key twice and locked the door. He sprinted downstairs and went outside. He entered the breakfast hall through the door right next to the hotel door. A heavy oily stench made his stomach churn. Swallowing several times, he thought, "It'll go away if I drink green tea."

He took his breakfast tray and set it on a table by the window. He went up to the horizontal cooler where all kinds of breakfast dishes were lined up and said to the middle-aged, plump red-cheeked woman on the other side of the cooler and said, "A large cup of green tea, please."

He took some sugar and a spoon from the counter while the woman poured his tea into the cup. After sitting in his chair and drinking a few sips of tea, he felt the swelling in his stomach dissipate. Feeling a sense of relief, he looked casually at the square from the wide window. Once again, both the bus stops in the square and the streets around the square were filled with vehicles. Smiling, he said, "It fills and empties like a bowl of water." He started eating his breakfast. While he was having breakfast, he didn't look anywhere until the last bite, as he did every day. Looking into the breakfast hall, he murmured "My goodness, this place fills up quickly," as he grabbed a coffee and sat back in his chair. Because the people in the breakfast room were talking loudly, the French and Dutch words they spoke seemed to be fighting with each other. For a while, he tried separating the words. When he realized that he wouldn't succeed, he forgot the words and the noise, and looked at the opposite wall. His gaze swept over to a framed photograph hanging on the wall. He turned her gaze to look at the other pictures again, but his gaze shifted and it stopped again on that photograph. After this was repeated several times, he looked more carefully at the photograph. Framed from a film frame, the photograph was not in color, but in black and white, and looked lively than the crumpled paintings in the painter's hand. There was also an inscription written in large letters underneath. He tried but was unable to read it with the naked eye. He put on his glasses that were sitting on the table. He looked at the text again and muttered, "Ruth Orkin." He squinted to read the rest of the text, "An American Girl in Italy," he said a bit loudly.

He was fed up with Ruth Orkin's provocative protruding breast strutting along the sidewalk, the Italian macho guys on the sidewalk oogling her as if they were going to eat her alive. Rather than laughing, he made a "hmh" sound through his nose. He took a few sips of coffee in quick succession. A guy standing a little ahead of Ruth Orkin with his jacket over his shoulder half-turned towards her caught her attention. Like the others, a guy was looking at Ruth Orkin walking along a busy street in Rome, but his stance gave the impression he was going to go chest-to-chest with the approaching Orkin.

What set the photograph apart from the others was that man's stance and Ruth Orkin's protruding strut. If it wasn't for one of them, that square would look like any of the other paintings and photographs on the wall. When he read the film's release date, he said, "his birth year," while feeling bitter joy.

He finished his breakfast in a hurry and reached for the cup to take the last sip of his tea when he saw the sign across the square. He peered carefully, as he had just done to read the text under the photograph. He looked again, as if he couldn't believe his eyes. He rushed out of the breakfast hall, leaving both the breakfast tray and the teacup on the table. He sauntered between the cars stopped at the traffic light and crossed to the opposite sidewalk. He turned and looked at the square, then the hotel room window, then the sign he had just seen. "Right across the room," he said happily.

He turned again to look at the hotel room window and the white inscription on the dark green background he stood near. His gaze swept back and forth between the window and the sign hanging over the door. "Even the sills are green," he said happily again, looking at the door under the sign. He stopped in front of the narrow door. He wanted to reach out and grab the door handle, but he didn't dare. He peered through the window by the door into the little shop with a furtive glance. He headed back towards the door. He still couldn't extend his hand. He looked at a bunch of ocher roses with green leaves drawn on the windowpane. In his embarrassment, he thought that his gaze fell on the serrated face of the cobblestones. He took a few steps away from the door. He started walking in front of the window, passing by it several times. He reached over to the doorknob several times. But he couldn't muster enough courage to grasp onto the door handle. Stepping away from the door, he looked back towards the hotel room. He saw her in the window of the room where he had just watched the square.

He muttered, "If only she wasn't here," as he thrust his hand into his pocket, fumbling for the room key. His heart broke once her fingertips touched the key.

Looking at the window, he said, "We stayed there in the first days after we arrived until we found a house."

His speech seemed to be stuck to his lips. He couldn't finish his sentence.

As if touching the white skin he had hidden in his mind, he uttered, "I've never loved anyone as much as you."

He realized that she'd succumb to his feelings.

"I wish you hadn't told me," she said in a voice he could hear, so that he could overcome his feelings by flaring up his anger to save his hollowed-out pride. His anger began to suppress his emotions, when he lifted his head and read the inscription, "Zaida the Florist" on the sign with a green background.

He took a few steps. Pausing, he looked at the sign

again, saying, "You've got your name spelled that way so they can say it easily."

He headed towards the door first, then took long strides to get away from it. He soon slowed down. His long strides became shorter. He stopped in his tracks, then turned back.

"A flower shop···" he said as he walked towards the door. He couldn't finish the sentence. He shut up angrily, his silence rising like a silent blast wave. He was sweating profusely. "It's all because of this fear," he said as he took a handkerchief from his jacket pocket and wiped his forehead. At such times, a single teardrop plopped into his palm. Bathed in tears, the lips of his long freckled face blinked. Turning her head so that she wouldn't hear the voice emitting from his lips, he heard the sentence, "I said I'd be a whore for a flower shop if necessary."

Glancing towards the shop, where he'd just walked away from, he asked, "Did you do that?" as he looked at the teardrop in his palm. His knees regained their strength.

"Quickly," he said, staring at the hotel room windows across the square. He sauntered away with long strides and came back in front of the door. He was reaching for the doorknob when the door opened. A woman emerged with a bouquet of flowers in her hand. Without looking at him, she hurried across the sidewalk and got into a car. She must've thought he wanted to enter, because she had left the door open. He peered intently inside, as if he wanted to see someone inside. He couldn't see anyone. Rereading the sign on the door, he stepped inside. He was excited to see the woman with her back turned amongst her flower pots and bouquets of flowers.

"Her braids," he whispered. He took two steps and paused. He then took two more steps. Pretending to look at the flowers, he glanced in the direction of the woman out of the corner of his eye. The woman on the other side of the counter was bent over. He couldn't see her face again.

Hearing the footsteps, the woman straightened up and looked at him, as he hurriedly asked, "Isn't she here?" The young woman looked carefully at this man she'd never seen before, "Who are you asking about?" she asked. The man realized that his courage was waning as he took a step back. Looking at the woman, he unconsciously whispered in his mother tongue, "Zaide Hanım…"

After a wry smile, the young woman said, "We lost my mother last year," looking at a customer who wandered into the shop.

Kidnapping in The Hague

He didn't even notice I was looking at him as he scanned the playing cards in his hand. He shifted his gaze slightly as he placed the deck of cards on the dark green felt tablecloth and looked at me. He winked when he saw me staring at him persistently. I half-turned back in my chair and bent over into his ear, and asked, "Do you know that guy?" I gestured with my head to the man sitting near the door.

He actually understood quite well whom I was referring to, but he still asked, "Which guy?"

I nodded again and pointed to the man I had just pointed out. I repeated my question as he looked indifferently in the direction I was pointing, like he wasn't interested.

"The guy sitting in the corner."

"This coffeehouse has four corners, and if you notice, you'll see there is someone sitting in every corner."

"I mean, the man sitting with his back against the column in the corner between the exit door and the window."

Looking ahead as if he didn't hear me, he pointed at the deck of cards with his big, long pointer, and said to his game buddy, "Cut," while sneaking a glance at the man I was referring to.

"He's a man like everyone else, with a different name, that's all."

I'd never seen him act so oddly towards me before. I

was totally taken aback by his behavior. Although I thought he probably didn't want to answer, I insisted anyway. "You see too, he's different from the others, he's not like everyone else."

"It seems separate at first glance, but if you look at him a couple of times and adjust your eyes, you'll see there's nothing that makes him stand out from anyone else."

"It may be so for you, but I don't think so. It seems he stands out from the others."

"It doesn't make much difference to me. Even if there's a difference."

As he uttered the last words of the sentence he left hanging, there was a tone I'd never heard before mixed in his voice. It was as if his voice was tied like a string in his throat and was getting hung up somewhere on the way out. I cut short the question in my mind when I realized he was having a hard time speaking. I looked at his face with a weary look, when he said, "If you look to look, he's no different from the others, but if you want to see something else, he's different," then went silent.

While I was thinking about how uneasy he was as well as the grumpiness spreading across his face, he glanced a few times at the man with his back to the support pillar in the corner of the coffee shop, grasping a cane tightly with one hand. He sighed, exhaling slightly different than he inhaled. He bit his thick, fleshy lower lip with yellowed upper teeth, and moistened his lips with his huge tongue that seemed like it could barely fit in his mouth. His lips trembled slightly as if he were going to say something, but stopped saying what he was going to say. He clenched his hand into a big fist, as if to vent his troubled anger, and needlessly smoothed the dark green tablecloth with both hands. He took the four cards his game partner had given him and stared at them for a long time. He changed their places a couple of times. After taking a deep breath, he annoyingly placed his cards on the table. While wiping the sweat from his brow with one of his large hands, he gestured the waiter for two glasses of tea with the other. He hadn't left unanswered any of the questions I've asked all this time, but I couldn't understand why he wasn't answering the question I asked about that man. While I was thinking, "There's no need to push," his partner, watching him from the corner of his eye, slowly picked up his cards. I thought to myself, "I'll ask one more time at the end of the game," my gaze shifting between the two. After looking at the cards in his hand, his partner looked at him with a smile: "Play already, if you're not going to play, let's throw in the towel," he said. Instead of playing, he just clenched his large hands into fists, then opened them and smoothed the tablecloth again. He took the cards from the table and stacked them in his palm. He combined the twos and eights from the four cards that had been laid on the table, put the ten in his hand on top of them and tied it at ten. Looking at his thick mustache, his partner laid the two remaining cards on the table saying, "I tied seven" on top of each other, and put the seven in his hand on top of them. He took the ten he had just tied as he bit his thick, meaty lips with his white teeth. His partner also took his sevens. He tossed the remaining four onto the table. His partner threw fives. No one has been able to tie any numbers. When he threw in the other cards in his hands, his partner gave four cards from the deck he took in his hand again. Seeing his distress escalated, I was annoyed that my question had flustered him so much. As soon as he picked up cards of the second hand, he smiled, trying to give me a gentle look. No matter how much he smiled, the anger in his eyes was evident. In fact, it was clear the anger in his voice and that in his eyes differed from each other.

He looked at the new cards in his hand, then at the cards on the table. He made a calculation in his head. Scratching his cheek with his free hand, he glanced at the sevens his buddy had picked up. He tied the nine on the table and put the nine from his own hand on top of it. After his buddy's play, he took the nines he had tied and placed them on the cards he had just picked up. Looking at his buddy's sevens from behind the same furious smile as before, he said, "You're going out." Giving him a sneering grin, his buddy took the nines he had just picked up with the nines in his hand and placed them over his own cards: "We'll soon see which of us is going out, won't we now?" he replied. While straightening his thick mustache, "Have you ever won this game?" he asked. "Maybe, but that doesn't mean I won't be defeated, does it?" "If you think you can win by getting three or five points like that, you're wrong!" "Look who's talking! You don't have much, either." He placed the nine in front of him. He reached out and took back all nine connected numbers his buddy had just taken. He feigned a chortle with his deep voice. When his laughter wore off, he blinked once or twice, looking at him with softened anger. "What's you talkin' about? What are these?" he said, pointing to the points he raked in. His pal wasn't the type to throw in the towel easily, either. After waving his hand in the air, he exclaimed, "You never know, look, they'll count towards me after a while." He waited for his friend's play without answering. When he played that card, he placed the last card in his hand over the nines he had taken, and with a swift movement, took the sevens lying in front of his pal. He chuckled, showing all his teeth, as he waited for his pal to deal the cards again. As if pissed off with his luck, his buddy snorted, "Laugh as much as you want, pal, but he who laughs last don't get joke." Without listening to his pal, he bellowed to the waiter, who was darting from table to table, "Hey, did you forget our tea?" As I stared at him, I blamed myself, still realizing that there was something forced about his movements. "I wish I hadn't asked him," I thought to myself. While I loitered around with such a feeling of regret, he played his game with a hand or two without uttering a word. Then, he chewed out the waiter who brought our teas, "Boy, I'm really glad we've got tongues to speak with, otherwise you'd forgotten all about us."

As the waiter wiped his hand on his work apron, he quipped, "I'm sorry, Yakup, man, as you see, it's packed today."

"I can see the place is packed, Recep, but you gotta take care of us in times like these. The others come around a few hours on the weekends, we're in here everyday. Some days we even forget to go home, but we don't forget this place, just so you can earn a living.

He wanted to say more, and tried to keep Recep at his side, but Recep wasn't having any of it. It was clear he was figuring something in his head as his eyes constantly wandered over the other customers.

As the waiter moved off, he grunted that the game didn't have much mojo left. Rocking slowly back and forth in his chair a few times, he looked over at his buddy.

After taking one last sip of tea in his glass, he said, "Dude, if you don't mind, I don't feel like playing anymore, I got the tea tab."

No sooner did he say that when he tossed his cards in his hand on top of the pile and called Recep over. In order not to get a similar earful of disdain that was lobbed at him a few minutes ago, Recep came over without further ado to the players with their big bellies flopping over the chairs and those watching Yakup looked up at him.

"Look how you just fly on over here whenever you want Recep."

He went silent for a while, then said, "Bring me our tab, so we can get the heck outta here. It's too crowded in here."

Fed up with all his ribbing, Recep retorted: "You don't have any tab."

Yakup smiled and looked at Recep's chubby, greasy face.

"My, don't you get bent outta shape in a hurry, Recep."

"No, man, I'm not bent outta shape, but this crowd just sort of flooded in outta nowhere today."

"Well, not to put them down, the poor buggers only have their weekends. You wouldn't see anyone here if they had residence permits to attend, Recep."

While saying that, he removed a tenner from his pocket and stuck it deftly into Recep's apron pocket. He stood up as he did that. Recep looked shiftily around, pretending not to notice the bill being stuffed in his apron. Gesturing with his hand, Yakup said gruffly, "C'mon, let's beat this popsicle stand."

As we made our way towards the exit, shoving the scattered chairs under the tables as we went, I couldn't help noticing the guy sitting in the corner by the door again. The man was sitting with his legs spread wide and his chin with its round beard resting on his cane, which he held with both hands. His belly and midsection were protruding over the chair. Seeing I was still interested in that man as we were walking out the door, Jacob suddenly grabbed my arm hard. He must have sensed the harshness of his movement, for as soon as we stepped onto the sidewalk, he loosened his grip a little. Before I could even look at his face, he took my arm. I gaped at him, assuming there was a reason for what he was doing.

When he saw me looking at him, he muttered, "Walk, just walk with me don't say anything!"

I've known him for years, but I've never seen him act like this way before. We were walking side-by-side without a word being said. After walking along the straight sidewalks for a while, we arrived at the spot where the first street splits. After turning the corner and walking down that street for a while, we went onto the main road. We still hadn't said a word to each other as we walked up to the traffic lights without speaking again. The light was red. I felt relaxed, waiting for it to turn green, but for some reason he was impatient. As soon as the light turned green, dragging me along in the process, we crossed the avenue. When he didn't slow down then, I asked him, "What's the hurry, Yakup? Where are we going?" He neither heard what I said, nor slowed his pace, let alone bother to even look at me.

This deep silence, which seemed interminable, continued until we reached the end of the avenue. We had just finished the avenue and turned the corner when he suddenly stopped in front of a door. "This door," he said, then took my arm again and walked away. We hadn't walked five steps before he stopped in front of a second door. "And this door," he said.

Looking down at the ground with his black eyes that were too wide even for his big face, he took a deep breath. As he exhaled, I thought his lungs would be expelled with his breath. He gestured as if to say something but said nothing. In a despondent tone that didn't match the tone of anger from just a few moments ago, he said, "Air travel wasn't easy back when we first arrived here. There were few flights and tickets were also quite expensive. At that time, there were buses coming and going back when. They used to depart from Topkapı and travel all the way here. Maybe it was a coincidence or just misfortune, call it whatever you want. When I got on the bus to come here, I met him while talking to folks sitting around me. Like me, he was headed to the Netherlands. When we learned there were a few others on the bus who were on their way to the Netherlands, we all decided to hire a car from Frankfurt to come here. We said to the bus driver, "You know these places, you know the way around, if you have any acquaintances, do us a favor and find someone who may want to drive us to the Netherlands." At first, the driver didn't warm up to the idea, but when we said, "we'll hook you up, too," from our first stopover in Germany, he phoned his bureau in Frankfurt to tell them to find someone. Someone with a car was waiting for us when we arrived in Frankfurt. The bus driver negotiated with the man. The man wanted practically as much as the bus fare between Istanbul and Frankfurt. We told them we couldn't pay him that much. This time, the driver negotiated for a better deal. The man looked at our bags. and we agreed on almost half of what he first wanted, saying "we haven't got much of a load." Actually, even that was too much. But we agreed, saying, "Let's pay a little more and be safe than sorry and get there with dignity." In fact, we noticed the bus driver and the guy were making a collusive bargain, but we didn't make a big deal about it.

We got in the car after we gave him money "for a cup of coffee," as he put it. As if the fee we paid him wasn't enough, we also covered his gas and smokes to boot. We just figured we paid the price for not knowing our way there. Anyway, that's all in the past.

I was so envious of the Mercedes the chauffeur drove to bring us here that day. That car roared along the German autobahns. Saying "there's still aways to go" every time we asked, the driver brought us to The Hague in five hours. He dropped us off in front of a coffeeshop where our people were sitting. He got up and left after we found folks at the coffeeshop who knew our acquaintances. After he left, our acquaintances immediately placed us in a hostel.

That day we shared the same room with him. Even when our homies found us a job in the same garden, we started commuting together. We got along like two brothers until we got our residence permits. We grew tired of staying in hostels, we wanted to get into a house, but because we didn't have residence permits, nobody was renting us houses. Anyway, we received residence permits in quick succession. We went together and signed up with the home office. After waiting about a year, he got the house which I'd just shown him, while I got this house, which we were standing in front of. The houses were small because they were built after the war, but we were so sick of the hostel that they seemed as big as palaces to us. Moreover, the rent was as much as we paid to stay at the hostel. We happily endeavored upon fixing the places up. We'd finish the repair work and cleaning, working in the garden during the day and on our homes in the evening. We furnished them in a manner we felt suitable. Sometimes we'd sleep at his house, other times at my house, we'd eat and drink, and sometimes we'd go to bars together in the evening. Most people thought we were brothers because they always saw us together. We were truly unbelievably best buddies. Our situation was steadily getting better in every regard. In our tourist days, not only we were working for the wages paid by the garden owners, half our earnings went to intermediaries. When we received our residence permits, we eliminated the intermediaries and our boss practically doubled our wage. We could hardly believe we had come here with just one suitcase each. But we didn't let that get to our heads. We also didn't forget our children. Beyond that, our longing for them loomed larger and larger.

After taking a breath and looking in the distance for a while, he began to soliloquize again, like I wasn't there.

"We had friends at work, at the coffeehouse, at the bar, but when we got home, we both fell into a loneliness indelibly etched into the void. For a while, after we had shoved the yearning into that void, we noticed some of our friends started to bring along their wives. But we couldn't decide right away because we couldn't overcome the thought inside us of going back. But after a few leaves of absence, we realized that we had grown accustomed to this place and that we'd never harbor the dream of returning. We decided to live together and bring our wives and children here. The year I bought my first car, before I went on leave, I completed the paperwork shortly and came back with my wife and children. After procrastinating for quite some time, he finally brought his wife and children. We had two kids and they had three. They were all small when they arrived here. His eldest and middle kids were girls and his youngest one was a boy. Both our wives hit it off immediately the day his children arrived. The younger ones were so-so, but the eldest girl was a stunner. As moment we saw her, we both thought she was an angel. She was very intelligent, and knew quite well how to make herself feel loved. As she attended school in the country for a few years, she was able she to learn the language in just a year while it took us five years to learn it. She surprised both us and her teachers. Thanks to her, we no freed from working as translators for women at hospitals and municipalities. She finished top of her class at both junior high and high school then she went on to study at university. We always considered her one of our own kids. She was both their daughter and our daughter. Well, the years went by as the kids grew up. By now, our homes had become too small for our shirts. We decided to buy a house for each of our wives, as the children started to study at high school. The banks were glad to make us loans as soon as they saw our payroll slips from our workplaces. We bought homes in different neighborhoods and moved away from each other. But Alev never broke away from us. She'd come to us every two days or once a week and share with us the joy she shared with her parents. We were doing our best to participate in her joy. You might not believe it, but we loved Alev even more than our children."

I couldn't quite figure out who he was talking about, whose children he was talking about?.

"Who was Alev?"

I looked in askance at his face, "Who are you talking about?"

He interrupted my sentence with a gesture. "Do you remember the man you showed me at the coffeehouse a while ago?"

"Yes, but what's this house have to do with him?"

He interrupted my sentence again. "Okay, if you remember, great. Now let me have my say first, then you can ask me whatever you want."

I nodded, trying to convey that I agreed with what he said and that I'd listen to him. But he wasn't looking at me. While I persistently cast my gaze on his face, he was looking towards the door of the house on the corner, saying, "Whenever Alev came out of this door you see, her friends waiting here on the street would be thrilled to see her. Because she'd start a game the moment she emerged, and she wouldn't let anyone pressure anyone else during the game. It was like she was the natural protector of our girls. That's how she completed primary school, laughing and playing. Our kids couldn't attend, but she went to the best high school after prep. Then she began university. It was there she befriended a young man as smart as herself. This young man was a doctor, who also went on to become an engineer. She talked to us about everything. She was the first to talk to us about the young man's marriage proposal. We told her not to rush into anything. Their courtship continued in relative silence for some time. In the end, they decided to get married. The boy's family came around and asked for Alev's hand. But the man you saw next to that door bit his tongue and didn't say "Yes." The young couple waited as patiently as was humanly possible. Once the hardboiled man said "No," he never regained the gumption to say "Yes." In the end, the couple's patience eventually ran out, because the two ran off and eloped. That's when damned Asim began to show his real colors. He mobilized all his relatives here and had them search for his daughter. But the search was in vain, as it seemed the couple had disappeared from the face of the earth. When he realized that he had searched for naught, he exclaimed that his petrified heart had softened and sent word to the couple via the young man's father. Meanwhile, Alev was pregnant. She was very happy her father had forgiven her. Like them, we were very happy that this affair was settled in this manner. When the young couple came around to kiss and make up, I was with them.

He said this to me, "Okay, I agree to everything, but my daughter has to leave my house as a veiled bride," he said to the young man··· Even though the young people said it wasn't necessary as they already had the municipality consecrate their matrimony, this stubborn ass of a man insisted. Alev consented so that he'd be willing too. She would be a guest at her father's house one week, and at the end of the week she would leave as a veiled bride to go to her own house. Preparations were made for a day or two. On the third day, a phone call came while we were all at their home, informing that Asım's father had died. We froze in our tracks. Asım told them to delay the funeral until he arrived. As it was, everyone was going to go on leave after the wedding. In these circumstances, they postponed the wedding until after their leave. Alev also took leave from her job and went along with them. We set out a few days after them. When we got back, Asım, his wife, middle daughter and son had returned, but Alev was nowhere to be seen. No one said anything about her. There was only a letter Asım had given the young man that he said he'd brought from Alev. According to what we learned from the letter, Alev had voluntarily married her uncle's son, writing that she'd never return to the Netherlands again. None of us believed it, but after years passed and no word about Alev was heard, we had no choice but to believe it, too. Nevertheless, we learned that not only was his father's death a ploy, but he had delivered his daughter, whom he said, "I gave her to my brother's son with my own hands," to the hangman with his own hands.

Doves

Neither the trees in the courtyard nor the tiled roof of the house could be seen from the high walls surrounding the property. When I turned the rusty iron handle of the street door and entered the courtyard covered with fruit trees, I heard my father muttered to himself, "Who knows what he did?"

As I walked towards the entrance door of the house, stepping on the stones laid between the trees, I muttered to myself, "I wonder whom did what to who." The voice of my father drowning out my voice, "They're like you and me," he exclaimed again.

He was standing on the small balcony a few steps above ground level, waving his walking cane and talking while looking towards the entry door of the house. He was so engrossed in his angry voice that he saw neither my entrance through the street door nor heard my deliberate footfalls. He paused as I approached the stairs, adding anguish to the soft anger in his voice, "God knows what you did to them?" he said once more.

Towards the end of his sentence, I noticed pain mixed with melancholy when his sad voice, soaked in anger, became thinner and softer. The pain he felt was no ordinary pain, but rather was as if a thin ache was mixed inside him. When I noticed that thin aching, I recalled my sister's voice I had heard years ago. My steps slowed. There was a tinge in his voice, not unlike the thin ache that had just blended into my father's voice. At that time, I was sitting on a cushion, reading a book on the balcony where my father is currently standing. As soon as my sister entered through the gate that I had just entered, she yelled, "Hey, bro!"

I got goosebumps the moment I heard her voice, as I tossed the book I was holding onto the stone flooring of the little balcony, stood up and walked over to my sister. When I got to her, she hurriedly wrapped her arms around my waist while trying to hold back her sobbing. When she managed to calm down a bit, she said again, "Bro, something terrible's happened!" then fell into sullen silence. Once she overcame her long silence, she started sobbing once more, saying, "Bro, Brunette Emine," in a voice ashamed to reveal a secret between us. While she tried stifling her hiccups, I thought of my Brunette Emine. On our last meeting, she pulled her warm palm away from my warm hand, wrapped her arm around my neck, and after placing an evasive peck on my cheek, said, as if addressing a murky street shadowed by high walls, "I've got a job now, Mustafa, so, I'll be taking all the stuff in our house until you finish school." Then she leapt up, took the kiss back that she'd just planted and ran towards their house at the end of the street. My mind set out towards a spring day as I gazed out from behind her silhouette blending into the shadow of the murky street.

We were playing in the school playground with our friends on that sunny spring day. My heart began to skip a beat when I spied a large yellow daisy at the foot of the playground wall. Without giving it a second thought, I went over, bent down quickly and plucked up the daisy. As soon as I got back up with the daisy hidden in my palm, I looked about for Emine. But when I couldn't see her anywhere, I freaked out, like a red poppy caught out in a strong gust of wind. As I said excitedly, "We were just running together," her soft voice exuded from behind me, "Were you looking for me?" she asked.

Until that day, although I wanted so much, I couldn't even say a word to make her sense my love, but she guessed I was looking for her when she asked, "Were you looking for me?"

Encouraged by her query, "Yes, I was looking for you!" I replied, as I hurriedly put the yellow daisy in her hand.

While hiding the daisy in her palm, she said, "I knew you were going to give it to me the moment you plucked it."

While I forced myself not to hug her, she wrapped her arms around my neck as if she were part of the game we were playing. Just as I was feeling the warmth of her body, she pulled back with an agile maneuver and sprinted off towards her friends.

After that day, we thought we'd be able to endure everything with the crazy wind of our fresh youth, and we promised each other things that even we ourselves couldn't believe. With the insane courage of that initial youthful breeze, after our final exam, we plunged into a grove of fruit trees adorned with pink shoots. As we walked hand in hand, our young lips had the pleasure of touching each other, and we wrapped our arms interminably around our newly inflamed bodies. Thinking our families would notice our absence, we promised to stay together regardless of what happened upon our return. In our senior year, Emine and I both earned spots at the boarding school, but her father objected, saying, "My daughter's not going on to school. This girl is already disobedient, and she won't listen to anyone if she goes on to college."

No matter how hard they tried, Emine and her mother couldn't convince her father to change his mind.

When we met the day before I departed for boarding school, she said woefully, "It's nice that you're going away to study."

In wishing to share in her sorrow, I said, "I wish you could study, too."

Without looking in my face, as if it was a continuation of her previous sentence, "Tell you what, I'll wait for you to finish school," she said. After a bit of reticence, she stubbornly said, "Who knows, maybe I'll find a job and work."

Encountering her obstinate voice, I forgot all that I was going to say and just hugged her waist with all my might instead. When my lips touched her freckled cheek, I became giddy with excitement as a heaviness descended over my heart. The fear that I'd suddenly lose her swept through my body faster than I could say "Jack Flash sat on a candlestick." When she hugged me, I realized her body was trembling like mine.

After a while, when our arms loosened involuntarily, she said once more with that stubborn voice of hers, "I'll wait patiently for you until you finish school," then hastily sauntered off.

For years, that departure she made in our final meeting has always shifted places in my mind. From time to time, my sister's voice saying the sentence, "Bro, something terrible's happened," mixed with the anguish in my father's voice, also interferes with her departures. At such moments, I can't differentiate whether she's leaving or my sister's speaking, but after my sister, who furiously entered the door, calmed down, "Bro, your brunette Emine is gone." She enthusiastically brought home a chicken given at the factory two days before. In sharing her enthusiasm, her mother cooked the chicken and set it on the dinner table. But her father, who was angry with Emine for getting a job without his permission, didn't even eat a bite of the chicken. As her mother didn't eat much of it, Emine went ahead and ate the rest of the chicken. Late that night, she began writhing in pain. Looking at her writhing daughter, her mother begged her father, but her father said, "Whenever she decides to listen to what her father has to say like other girls and promises to sit at home and wait on her fate, that's when I'll take her to see the doctor."

When neither hair nor hide was heard from Emine towards last night, her mother said, "If you're not going to take her, then I'll take her to the doctor," then she hoisted Emine onto her back. But Emine's condition worsened even before they got through the hospital entrance. The doctors and nurses came running, but they couldn't save Emine. Beating the side of Emine's coffin at her bedside in their house, her mother had the last word, finishing her words by saying, "It's all because of this man's stubbornness··· Because of this man's stubbornness··· Beating her chest and screaming, "My Emine left us because of this man's stubbornness!" she was caught in a fresh shower of tears.

Years ago, my sister went to the other side like my brunette Emine. What she said that day, her crying at that moment, and her face disappeared by mixing with other words, other faces and other crying in my mind, but as soon as I entered the door, the thin aching mixed with the anguish that was hidden in her voice remained in my heart as she said, "Bro, something terrible happened." It's because of that anguish I think I always sleep at night with Emine in the bed I go to with Ayşe, my wife of 30 years.

I climbed the stairs to the balcony and got up real close to my father. I was going to reach out my hand and grab it when, "They want to feel love too," he said. He stopped when he saw my hand reaching towards him. As he hurriedly waved his cane from side to side, he asked. "Did you see what your mother did?"

I was quite intrigued. What had she done to make him suffer so much?

"No, I haven't seen or heard anything about it. What did my mother do?"

My father added fury to his aching voice, "What more could she have done?"

While holding his arm to calm him down, I said, "Sit on the chair, take two breaths and tell me what my mother did to you?"

After breathing through his nose, he retorted, "There's no way I can sit and look, my whole body trembling."

I straightened the cushion on the wooden chair in the middle of the balcony. I took his wrinkled, bony hands and helped him to slowly sit in the chair. As he tightly clutched his cane, as if to hide his trembling hands, he said, "She bitches at me every time I go from one room to another."

Combining his silence with his dull, greyish-blue eyes, he looked at me. After wetting his thick lips with his tongue, he said, "Bring me a glass of water, I'm extremely thirsty,"

I brought him a glass with the pitcher I filled from the tap. He looked at the glass jug of water in my hand and then at me. Saying dubiously, "Did you just fill it up? I won't drink that water if it's your mother's jug from last night."

Hearing what he said, I was shaken by a shudder I

hadn't felt in years. My mom must have done something really bad, for dad to be so angry with my mom with whom she shared the same pillow for over 60 years. In order not to think about that terrible thing, I looked up at the vine we call the "bride's finger," which had sprung from a single root and spread all over the yard, and other fruit trees my father had grown. I saw he was still hesitant about drinking the water when I plucked my courage again and turned my gaze towards my father. Raising my voice to help him decide, I reassured him, "I just filled it, it's not from last night."

While taking the glass he held with both hands to his mouth, he squinted his greyish-blue eyes, and in a slow voice, said, "Sit on over next to me."

I sat on the top rung of the few steps to the little balcony, close to his knees. I looked at my father. When he realized I was waiting for him to drink the water and explain to me, after rushing to drink the water and handing me back the glass, with a high-pitched voice coming out of his throat, he said, "The water was really fresh." Looking in my face for a while longer, he leaned against the back of his chair. "See that stone?" he asked, pointing to the black mortar stone in the garden with his cane. For a while, I looked at the black mortar stone that my sister in Germany brought back while she was on leave in the trunk of her car from my grandfather's village, which is now in Bosnian territory.

Wondering where this was leading to, I said, "I see."

According to us, that stone was a black stone not unlike other black stones. But you couldn't imagine how happy my father was whenever he saw that stone. Forced to walk with a cane, that man literally jumped into the air the day he saw that stone. After bending down and kissing this stone, he shouted, "I can now die comfortably."

As I looked at him that moment, I understood why he had begged us for years to "take me to my village once." It turned out that all he wanted was to see a part of his childhood. In his own words, my father died "comfortably" shortly after seeing that stone. I answered him but he was still looking at me. Assuming he didn't hear me, I said once more, "I see the mortar stone, Dad."

His voice had softened. In that soft voice, he stated, "After you left home, it was just me and your mother. I was looking everywhere for a little bit of your childhood as well as mine. But I was aware I was getting more and more lonely. To rid myself of that solitude, I started talking to my trees in the garden I'd planted years ago. Dealing with the soil was tiring my old body, but it also did me a lot of good. I started to feel a sneaky weariness filling me while I was preoccupied with my trees. I was about to let myself go when your sister brought this mortar stone. I talked with it a lot in those days of exhaustion. In those days, the two of them came together. They were devastated by the heat. They looked very tired. They were obviously very thirsty. I immediately filled the mortar with water, which they guzzled down.

After quenching their thirst, they took a splattering bath with the remaining water. Thinking they were hungry, I cut the half a loaf I brought from home into small pieces and tossed it in front of them. But they continued to play with the water and didn't even eat a single piece. Ever since that first day, I started to come and wait for them at the same time. If they were a little late, I'd fall into a funk, repeating "what's taking them so long?" Whenever I came around to drink their water, I was talking to them. Last week, when I fell ill and couldn't get out of bed, they offended your mother. I kept telling her to fill the mortar stone with fresh water and cut the bread into small pieces. But I just wasn't getting through to her…"

I stared at him for a while, as if I didn't understand who he was talking about. When he didn't say anything, I asked., "Who offended my mother?"

Looking up at the blue sky with those bright greyish-blue eyes of his, my father said in an anguished voice, "Who else was it going to be, the doves, of course," he said.

Wilma's Treasure Trunk

She still couldn't get over her anxiety as she walked over to the closed curtain. When she got to the window, she stopped suddenly. She pulled back the curtain and looked out. For a while, she watched the dark red rays of the sun, trying to hide behind the roofs of the houses on the opposite side of the street, turning purplish as they mingled with the blue of the sky.

Turning her gaze back to the street, she grimaced as if she had lost hope. In a soft, gentle yet hopeless voice, she said, "There's no one in sight." As she let go of the faded brown velvet curtain she held with one hand, the room was filled with gloomy darkness that spelled high anxiety once more. She was startled out of her wits in the dark. Hastily lighting one of the crystal glass lamps in the ceiling, jubilant lights emanated from shards of crystal glass filling the square living room, gleaming on the polished walnut furniture. Scanning the living room with an invariable dull look that had been in her eyes for days, she spotted the walnut chest that had been sitting on a wheeled coffee table for years and looked like it was one piece. Her forehead was full of wrinkles. Hearing the sound of a car coming from the street, she hurried to the window. She opened the middle-parted curtain to both sides. A lazy, troubled tiredness came over her as she looked again at the street, which was preparing to be thrown into the arms of the evening coolness, and saw no one.

In a voice that didn't stray far from her lips she said, "As always, they're not going to keep their word this time, nor will they be showing up."

She realized her weariness when he felt a thin pain descending from her thick legs to her feet. She trundled slowly and sat down on a worn leather armchair that was peeling in places. Unable to withstand the weight of her wide hips, the armchair collapsed. She stood up, clutching the edge of the chair, reeling backwards. A bitter smile raced across her face as she stared at the armchair. She murmured, "Perhaps the trunk's rotten like these pieces. The lid's probably going to yank right off."

As she timidly walked over towards the chest, her gaze fell on the two dried red roses in the Delft blue porcelain vase in the middle of the light brown round table. She glanced at a rusty key beside the vase. For a moment, her gaze hovered between the chest and the key.

Turning her head, as if ashamed of what she had thought, she encountered the door to her bedroom, which was always open. Shaking her oversized hips, she entered her bedroom through the open door and lit the lamp. Inside was a wide bed, a heavy, bulky closet against the wall directly opposite the bed, and a make-up table that had stood in the same spot next to the wardrobe for years. Like the round table in the living room, they were light brown, close to red. There were lipsticks, blushes, and assorted cream boxes on the vanity table. She was overcome with a feeling as if she was doing something sinful as she stretched out her hand towards a tin of cream. After a moment of hesitation, she withdrew her hand. Her ears rang; she thought the doorbell was ringing. Holding her breath, she listened outside. Hearing no sound, bitter anxiety came over her face again. She went over and sat down in a chair that was leaning against the wall at the head of the bed. She looked at the wide bed from where she was sitting. A hollow smile crept across her lips, as she brushed his long blonde hair back, shaking her head like she did whenever she was bothered. She leaned her back against the back of her chair and her head against the wall behind the chair as her grandmother's wrinkled face floated before her eyes. She followed her for a while. She rolled her eyes up to the ceiling. She had the feeling her grandmother's big green eyes were staring at her from all over the ceiling. Her thoughts oscillated between fear and joy as her mind was shattered in smithereens. She closed her eyes only to be awakened by the warmth of the tears running down her cheeks. She remembered coming to visit her grandmother a few weeks ago.

While she was treading lightly in her memories, she said, "I'd just entered through the outer door. I couldn't tell if she my footsteps or if it was the fresh air coming in that woke her up."

She called hoarsely, "Mari, come over to me quickly." I ran to her without even closing the outer door. She laid still, as usual.

Leaning towards her, I said, "Grandma." Her manner of laying in bed without any reaction worried me, but I still wanted to cheer her up a little, so I kidded her, "Grandma, you look like you weren't expecting me, or maybe you were expecting someone?"

She looked in my face. Trying to smile forcibly, she said in a shrilly tone despite her dull eyes, "Everyone in this world loves one who's standing, baby. But even their own children don't visit her when a person's stuck in bed.

After an icy silence, she slammed her hand on the edge of the bed, saying, "Come sit next to me."

"Grandma, let me put water on the stove for coffee first and then I'll sit down," I said.

"Never mind the coffee," she replied with a wink, "You can do that later, sit next to me now."

It was the first time I had seen her so calm after her painful bout of internal bleeding. She gestured for me to come closer to her. I moved my chair a little closer to the bed. I took her wrinkled hands into my large ones. A soft, rosy bliss spread over her broad freckled face as her old, cold hands warmed in my warm ones.

Pointing with her finger to the chest on top of the cart, visible from the open door, she said, "I was little. My grandfathers, who lived in a village close to the city where my father worked, had a long field. My grandparents had a big house in the middle of the field. The field was always surrounded by a narrow water-filled ditch.

My grandfather had gardened half of the field. The remaining section was cattle pasture and a vegetable garden. The railway passed through the south side of the field. My parents and I used to go to my grandparents practically every weekend. Whenever we went to that house, I'd eagerly run towards the tracks the moment I heard the sound of the train. However, each time the train rushed by before I could even reach the edge of the canal. Whenever the train passed by like that, I thought the cows grazing in the field were laughing at me, and I'd start crying and that would be almost always the same. One day, when the green grass was smiling up at the hot sun and there wasn't a cloud in the clear blue sky, my mother began running after me to catch me while I ran exuberantly towards the tracks again. With that chase, we'd reach the edge of the ditch before the train passed. As soon as we arrived, we'd start waving to the passengers on the train, which was continuing on its way, trailing a plume of black smoke. Some of the passengers who saw us waving also waved at us. I really enjoyed the way we and the passengers waved to each other like that. As the train pulled away, my mother hugged me and lifted me into the air. I was still chortling with joy. As my mother gently laid me on the grass, she said, 'You know, your grandfather is coming from Paris by this train. Your father went to meet him in a horse-drawn buggy a little while ago.' The weather was very warm. We were both thirsty when we got home.

First my mother drank water, then she gave it to me. She didn't want to stay indoors because of the hot weather. I went out again. There were many trees whose names I don't know in my grandfather's backyard garden. I mostly liked the rustling leaves of these fruit trees, whose names I didn't know, when the wind hit, and when I heard that rustling, I fell into a sweet slumber. That's what happened that day. My father's deep, nasal voice awoke me, 'Wilma, Wilma.' When I barely woke up from that sweet sleep and opened my eyes, I saw my grandpa, who was taller than my father, standing behind him. His blond hair, which had turned half white, was combed back as usual. He grinned with his blue eyes, and said as he handed me a wrapped chocolate bonbon, 'I brought this back from Paris for you, Wilmacik,' as he winked.

"While I was busy ripping off the shiny paper off the chocolate, my father said again in his deep, full voice, 'You didn't thank Grandpa.' Instead of thanking him, I gave them both a kiss and then a piece of my chocolate. Grandpa must have liked it so much that he did something he had never done before and took me in his arms. That day, when I entered the house on Grandpa's lap, I saw this chest placed in a corner of the living room. He told me, 'All that remains from my grandmother to my mother, from my mother to me, and from me to you is in that trunk.'"

Those last words stretched a little between her lips.

The thin fingers inside my large hands moved meaningfully. Her upper lip twitched for a while. When the twitching subsided, she began relating how she separated from her first husband.

"He, like the others, also caught the bug of going to New Zealand. After returning from the military, he said, 'I'm going' practically every evening. I was pregnant with your uncle. Even though I told him not to go, he was talking incessantly, night and day, about the farm he was going to set up in New Zealand. He said he'd send for me and the kids once he had it set up. But after he left, I never heard from him nor his farm. Maybe he died on the way before he even got there. Your mother and aunt grew up and got married. Your uncle left home as soon as he turned 18. When they left, I was left alone. At first I loved solitude, but when it got too unbearable, I married a second time. My children resented me for getting married. The man I married died years ago, but my children's selfish resentment still hasn't passed. They haven't opened my door for years. Maybe I'll die with their longing··· But Mari. Me too···"

She didn't finish the sentence. After an interminable silence, she looked at me with her dull eyes and said, "I told the doctor. If my bleeding starts again like last time, he's going to have to boost the morphine and it'll all be over. I don't want to go through that pain again, Mari··· Anyways, I don't think my weak body could endure it," she said, with a look pleading me not to interfere with the doctor.

Marianna's tears mingled with her grandmother's green gaze when the doorbell rang hastily several times. Marianna hurriedly ran towards the door as she wiped away her tears. As soon as she opened the door, her uncle, aunt and mother entered, one after the other.

Her mother, uncle, and aunt took seats on three chairs with finely handcrafted backs that surrounded the round table in the living room. Marianna went and retrieved the chair in her bedroom and came back. They sat for a while in silence, without looking at each other. Marianna was praying for someone to start the conversation when her aunt, who was very bored, said coldly. "We didn't come here to sit. Let's get it over and done with. I've got to get to work early in the morning."

In a voice similar to her sister's, Marianna's mother added, "I haven't got much time either.".

Her uncle pursed his lips, as if offended by what his sisters were saying. With a distressful gesture, he took a cigarette from the pack in his hand and lit it. Marianna asked her uncle for a cigarette to dissipate this burdensome, mute air. Lighting the cigarette her uncle gave her, she took a few puffs in quick succession. It was as if she was suffocating. Tears filled her eyes, but she smoked it stubbornly down to the end. While crushing the butt in the ashtray, she heard her uncle say, "Marianna, you've been taking care of Mother how many years now, what do you have to say?"

Her uncle's voice was as booming as it was far away from her. It probably wasn't this uncle who had a soft heart who visited her grandmother once in a while. While Marianna was looking to see if it was really was her uncle's voice emitting from those lips, she heard the voice of her aunt, who was younger than her mother and came to visit her grandmother every couple of years.

Her aunt said, "I don't want hear about this. Marianne was coming to see Mother for herself. It's all clear, let's get this inheritance business over as soon as possible."

Without saying a word, Marianna took the rusty key off the table and handed it to her uncle. Her uncle turned the key over in his fingers for a while. He glanced at his sisters and Marianna several times. Realizing Marianna had no intention of talking much, he got up and wheeled the cart holding the hand-carved chest to the side of the table. He opened the lock by inserting the key and turning it three times. From the opened chest, the scent of lavender soaked in mothballs wafted into the room. While everyone looked at one other, Marianna's uncle reached into the trunk and pulled out an ancient tiny Virgin Mary icon, three mother-of-pearl buttons, three silk blouses, one white, one yellow and one pink, a half-burned red candle, a World War II medal, a sailor's cap and placed them all on the table.

Looking indifferently at the items on the table, Marianna's mother asked, "Is that all there is?" Without replying, her uncle reached into the chest and pulled out an envelope, which he handed to her mother.

In a thoroughly cold voice, he added, "There's this as well."

Marianna's mother hastily opened the envelope and removed a folded sheet of paper.

It said plainly:

> *"My whole existence is this house in which I live and the belongings it holds I bequeath it all to my granddaughter Marianna van Zevendıjk, who patiently took care of me in my last years.*
>
> *(01.04.00) Wilma van der Schauduw"*

Marianna's mother gasped several times with anger and disbelief. She hurriedly tossed the paper over the other items as if the paper had soiled her hands. While Marianna's aunt expressed her displeasure in this behavior, her troubled gaze scanned the room several times. For a while, she stared at the chest with a walnut leaf design carved onto it.

Pointing to the paper next to other items, she said, "This writing's not my mother's." Marianna was ashamed of her aunt's accusation, squirming with the desire to hide her tall, large body somewhere else.

Frustrated, she said, "Auntie, you know darn well this

is Grandma's writing. That said, I served her voluntarily and lovingly. She wrote that all right, but I don't want anything from her, I would appreciate it if you would just give me this chest as an heirloom from Grandma."

After fluttering her long eyelashes, her aunt said without altering her tone of voice, "Even if it's my mother's letter, I don't think this letter has any value. Both the house and the trunk are going to be sold off and the income will be shared amongst us three siblings."

While Marianna's uncle remained reticent, her mother spoke in her sister's voice, "Maybe the trunk's got some antique value," she said.

Roberto Bienco

Leaning on the cane in his hand, he first put one foot forward, then slowly brought the other foot to his side. He proceeded to the driver, relying on his cane, to which he had attached a rubber stopper to deaden the sound at the bottom end. He slowly pulled out his wallet from his inside jacket pocket. He counted the coins he poured into his palm and handed them to the driver. He looked resentful at the way the driver carelessly tore his ticket off the stub and handed it to him. Along with the coins remaining in his palm, he stuck the ticket in his wallet, and shoved it back in his jacket pocket with the same anger. Leaning with one hand on his rubber-tipped cane, he took two big steps towards the middle door of the bus, grabbing onto the safety bar with the other. He turned his dark yellowish-hazel eyes to look towards the back of the bus, fluttering his long eyelashes. Whether it was because he was blinking his eyelashes or because his dark complexion was deceiving us, his large pupils sparkled like a cut diamond held up to the light. He stopped as he approached the middle door, then turned halfway to look at the driver with thinly-veiled anger. Leaning forward slightly, he spread his legs wide, then looked at his walking stick.

Extending his hand to us as he held onto the bar he said loudly, "Roberto Bienco"

His voice, his posture, his eyes, his dark tanned skin, his worn-out, seedy jacket, were reminiscent of a theater actor who had a major case of stage fright, who wanted to say what he couldn't say on stage. He stuck his index finger into the void, muttering what was on his mind with his moving lips. In a loud voice, inflating the dark veins in his wrinkled neck, he repeated aloud again, "Roberto Bienco."

Inhaling hard, he puffed up his broad chest as if he had exhausted all his breath, wetting his lips with his fat tongue. He slammed his rubber tipped cane hard twice on the bus floor, as he breathed visibly once more.

Scanning the passengers on the bus one by one with luminous eyes, he said in a similar tone, "You don't know Roberto Bienco," and fell silent, as if he had been tranquilized. His silence was eerily like that of an eagle's wings soaring over his prey. Somehow he managed to heave that dreadful silence over us as well. We got goosebumps.

Despite the goosebumps or whether we were listening or not, he related his tale:

Roberto Bienco would get up in the morning, first look at the silvery sun peeking out from behind the green hills, then listen to the sound of the wind whistling through the trees. On that last day, after kneeling in front of the sun, he began listening to the wind whispering through the trees. While he was repeating what the wind was saying, he watched as a green snake came slithering towards him from the bushes with a shining gaze in his coal black eyes.

When the snake reared up and added his voice to the sound of the wind, his dark complexion began to turn white with fear. As the green serpent slithered by, he said to himself, 'Boy, you shouldn't go out of the hut today.'"

He fell silent, as if measuring the impact of what he was saying. He blinked, his long eyelashes fluttering. Leaning on his rubber-tipped cane decorated with snake figures, he took a step toward the middle door, then toward the front door. He swept his gaze over us with lightning speed. Not quite fathoming the impact of what he was saying, he frowned.

After pausing a while, he continued:

You don't know Roberto Bienco. You don't understand what I was saying either. To understand, you have to look backwards in time. Because back then, the calendar of African tribes was the sun and they had no temples. The sons of the corpse were also covered in clay and were locked in the trunks of Baobab trees before they died. At that time, what your ancestors called jinn was called rab and pangol by the black-skinned people of green Africa. Rabs and pangols also demanded live sacrifices every year in exchange for not committing evil. The tribes would sacrifice one of the valiant warriors of the tribe, or the most beautiful girl of the tribe so they wouldn't commit evil. The day Roberto Bienco said, 'Boy, you shouldn't go out of the hut today' was one of the days when such a sacrifice ceremony would be held. Fresh game meat was also required for the ceremonial presentation of the sacrifice. So as not to frighten the hunters and warriors, Roberto Bienco didn't tell anyone he saw the green snake. Roberto Bianco had forgotten he had seen the green snake as the sun rose and the hunters and warriors of the tribe, went into the dark forests to hunt. Warriors and hunters proceeded to the shore of the great waters, hiding their catches in nooks and crannies where predators couldn't find them. Unable to endure the scorching heat, the young warriors ran and saw the sailing vessels bobbing on the waves as they were cooling off in the salty bosom of the great waters. They started swimming towards the shore the moment they saw it, but those on board the sailing vessels had already launched their lion-headed lifeboats, as they had seen them before.

While the young warriors and hunters were swimming, the blue waters approached the shore at lightning speed. The lifeboats approached the shore as the warriors and hunters, who thought it was a game, were running between the dense trees. Before the warriors and hunters could even take cover, toys that shone brightly in the hands of those who disembarked from the lifeboat began to vomit fire. The tallest of those who disembarked from the lifeboat was striding in front, firing nonstop.

While the warriors and hunters looked at each other in shock, Roberto Bienco's heart was weeping when he heard the sound of the forest, "The green snake warned you in the morning" conveyed by the wind.

Seeing him crying, the tribal chief crawled up to him and whispered, "Warriors don't cry, Roberto. These are red-bearded pangols from the sea. But until now, I'd never seen or heard red-bearded pangols making popping noises with their shining toys in their hands."

He spoke in a whisper, but the old warrior who was an adept lip reader comprehended quite well what the chief was saying. The poor man's hands trembled as the red-bearded pangol repeated the words, as his arrow dropped to the ground. Hearing the voices, the red-bearded pangols began to fire more fiercely than before towards the warriors.

As a hail of bullets was mowing down the young saplings, a desperate tribal chief pleaded to Roberto, "You're the fastest and bravest of my warriors, take someone with you. Sprint to our village. We don't stand a chance of being rescued, but at least you can save them."

Then he bestowed him with an order of leadership so the tribe would believe what Roberto Bienco told them. Roberto Bienco and the friend he took with him became the wind as they plunged into the dense trees. At that moment, it was as if the sky split open *and all the lightning bolts of the gods struck the warriors. The warriors were so frightened after that explosion that they hugged the ground. Once they were stuck on the ground, red-haired pangols proceeded over to them and strung them up on a rope like a rosary.*

While two armed pangols were waiting for warriors and hunters, who were lying naked on the hot sand, the leader of the red pangols and the others fell behind Roberto Bienco and his friend with their strong legs. They couldn't keep up with Roberto Bienco and his friend, but a tigress suddenly leapt on them from amongst the dense foliage, halting Roberto and his friend.

After a fierce struggle, Roberto Bienco thrust his poisoned arrow into the tiger's belly, while the tiger plunged his teeth into the throat of Roberto Bienco's friend with all his might.

That's when Roberto Bienco heard the footsteps of the approaching pangols not far behind. He left his blood-covered friend with the tiger and began running again at lightning speed. Before long, the pangols saw him, but he couldn't see them because he wasn't looking back. He was in the front, while the pangols arrived in the village in the back. But as Roberto Bienco approached, he shrieked and shouted to the villagers in the huts, "Run for your lives!" A few villagers managed to escape thanks to his warning.

However, quickly cutting off the escape route, the red-bearded pangols *didn't allow anyone to escape. After torching the huts of the elderly and sick, they tied the women, girls, children and men lying on the ground by their arms. Roberto Bienco, whom they caught by throwing a net over him, was pulled out of the net and tied to the ground rope as well. He risked death when he removed a poisonous arrow he kept in a small wooden box carried around his chest with a cord twisted from tree bark, and blew it in the face of the tallest pangol.*

As he cried in pain, the pangol started beating Roberto Bienco, but the poison was so powerful that by the third hit, his arm stiffened and remained suspended in the air.

Seeing him die frothing at the mouth, the other pangols *swooped down on Roberto Bienco. However, the chief of the red* pangols *shot into the air.*

And when his men came to their senses, he admonished them, "Do you want to kill the man who's worth the most money, you boneheads?" Then he said, "C'mon, let's toss Hans' body into the fire." While Hans' greasy body was burning side by side with the corpses of the elderly and infirm, the bound peasants and red pangols *set off towards the great sea.*

Once the convoy reached the chained warriors, the women with their hands tied became worse than ti-

gresses when they saw their chief captured. For a moment, the pangols were totally confused. But the moment they came to their senses, they grabbed their guns and started shooting at the stars. Petrified by the noise, the village women threw themselves on the hot sand.

The tribal chief alone first turned his face towards the sun, then shrieked, "O forgive me, great light! I must die first as I can't protect my tribe from this evil from the great sea, the mother of the red pangol!" and started screaming bloody murder.

The pangols, who couldn't silence him, untied his hands first and then shot him dead in front of his tribe. While their chief was lying in a pool of blood, they transported their captives to their lion-headed sailboats in lifeboats.

They tied the captives tightly by their arms and legs to iron rings nailed to the masts in a basin half-filled with water. The sailing vessels pulled up anchor and got underway. Unaccustomed to sea travel, it wasn't long before the captives became seasick. They vomited in the water they were submerged in up to their waists. The water of the pool fluctuated with the rocking of the sailboat. With the rippling water, the vomit spread throughout the pool and stuck to the bodies of the prisoners. Suspended into the water in a net, Roberto Bienco's body was covered in vomit.

The red-haired pangolins were in a good mood but

were angered by Roberto Bienco's screams, which hadn't subsided since he was hoisted on board. Although he was whipped several times, Roberto Bienco was still raising a racket. Finally, the leader of the red pangols had him tossed into solitary confinement.

One day, the awful clanking machines suddenly stopped operating. For a long time there was a deafening silence. It was the voice of the chief of the red-bearded pangols that broke the silence. The prisoners were removed one by one from the pool and laid out on the deck with their vomit encrusted bodies. After being kept under the sun for a while, they were hosed down with pressurized water.

They looked a bit human-like once their blackened bodies were cleansed. However, while Roberto Bienco, whom they still couldn't silence, had his hands bound and his feet chained, the others were tied together with only a rope and taken to a lock-up. While the prisoners, who were kept waiting for days in that warehouse in the port of Rotterdam, set out to go to their new owners' vessel on a sunny day, new pangols who didn't recognize Roberto Bienco set him free. Roberto Bienco jumped on the pangol that untied his hands with a cry that was as heartwarming as his first cry. Not knowing his objective, the new pangol panicked and withdrew a dagger from his waist and plunged it in Roberto Bienco's belly. As his eyes grew *cold, Roberto Bienco's countenance bore a happy glint of being freed of his embarrassment. He didn't voyage to Surinam, but the captive people of his tribe took his song with them to the land where I was born. The lines passed down from those days are still sung in those parts:*

> *"Roberto's eyes were like fire, as he ran like the dickens. His voice pierced like a dagger as he shrieked, 'run for your life'."*

My grandmother always sang this song of her great-grandfather. He's the one who gave me my name Roberto Bienco so I could be a valiant warrior like his great-grandfather. I just gave this name to my granddaughter who was born today.

Honor

He was running breathlessly down the wet sidewalk. His only goal was to arrive at the police station at the end of the street, and once there, to unflinchingly begin relating his heroism by saying, "I leaned against the wall, and aimed right at his head."

While running like that, he slowed down a little in front of the coffee shop where he hung out every day. He peered through the large window, his eyes squinting. Almost all of his acquaintances were there, and they drifted away from their real world as usual and immersed themselves in the exciting world of card games. None of them saw him staring into the window as he passed by. He must have been a little resentful that nobody saw him, because he said, "You'll all hear about it soon enough," as he started running faster than before.

His lungs expanded as he quickened his pace, and he was wheezing as he ran. These noises must have been a sign of his heroism, because heroism wasn't that easy. Surely there must have been some signs. A little later, when he reached the police station, he was going to say, "I leaned against the wall, aimed right at his head, and pulled the trigger without trembling…" That's because the fact his hand didn't tremble was also a sign of his heroism. Within an hour, all of The Netherlands, perhaps all the world's agencies would reflect his heroism to the radios, televisions and newspapers. The news about them would be announced in the newspapers, on the radio, and on the television. He had to express himself heroically, without trembling hands, legs, and lips. He had to give such an impression so that his father and mother, who had forbid all his rights, should have been proud of him. Whatever the entire world was, his father needed to be aware of his heroism. Because if he wasn't made aware, he wouldn't be right again. He couldn't walk with his head held high unless he gave his right.

Having planned everything heroically, Mesut opened the third button of his blood-spattered shirt as he entered the police station to suit his heroism. He wanted to show the black hairs of his chest, another sign of his heroism. He shoved his hands in his pockets as soon as he walked through the revolving glass door. He proceeded to the information desk with slow, heroic steps. There was no one behind the high wooden bench. He leaned his chest against the bench. As his gaze scanned the walls, he took a few breaths, expelled the air from his lungs and put his elbows on the bench. While he waited with his head in his hands, the image of Yeli hit the opposite wall. While looking at her, Yeli in the image started to dance beautifully, curling her hips with the master belly dancers.

Resentful of her dancing like such an artist, Mesut frowned thickly and laughed under his moustache, "You can't dance anymore."

Yeli laughed as well, replying, "I can if I want."

As soon as she said that, she started dancing with her

belly rather than her hips. Although she noticed he was angry, she came up to Mesut and took his big hand.

"C'mon, join me," she said, pulling him towards her.

Taken aback Mesut pushed her back with his hand, "I danced with you once in my life. No, I'm really not a good dancer, I just shake my butt. And that was at our wedding, too. Back then, you were dancing the do-si-do very well, too. But more than dancing, I was looking at you and trying to touch you more. I even wanted to hug you, fill my arms with you, and water the dryness of years inside me with your lips. No, I wanted to kiss you to the fullest, not an escapade like with that photographer. But not when everyone's eyes were on us. Jeez, Yeli, if only you had stayed as you were when you first pierced my heart!" he said breathlessly.

While speaking with the image of Yeli on the wall, he clutched his head between his palms so much that his ears hurt. With the pain in his ears, he recalled where he was again.

When he thought of his heroism again, he smacked the high bench with his fist. "I don't need Yeli anymore," he cried in a deep, heroic voice. But nobody heard him shout. Like all heroes, he snorted for a while, and got hot behind his ears. The tip of his nose ached. Just as a drop of tear was streaming down his lashes, he whimpered, "I'm not going to cry no matter what!" as he saw the tear running down his eyelashes fall onto the bench. He fell reticent when he saw the teardrop. As he stood in such silence, he noticed his legs were trembling. He put all his weight on his elbows when he realized he was afraid of what was going to befall him. Or rather, he dropped himself on his elbows. But it didn't help. His trembling got even worse. He gripped the wooden bench tightly with his hands. That didn't help matters either as tremors engulfed his entire body. His hands were untied, and just as he was about to drop to the ground, one of the yellow doors, which appeared to be embedded into the wall opposite, opened slowly, a tall, blond female policeman who emerged in the room. Mesut began crying aloud before she could ask him anything.

The policewoman was surprised at what was happening.

Running from behind the counter, she attempted to grab Mesut by the arm with her long-fingered hands, asking, "What happened, sir, why are you crying?"

Hearing the lady policeman's voice, which was similar to Yeli's, Mesut totally caved in and started bellowing like an ox. The policewoman started shaking him in an effort to calm him down.

In a soft, slow voice, she said, "Please don't cry, sir." Mesut wept quite a bit, then sniffled a few times. He sobbed a couple of times. When his crying subsided, she grabbed his arm and lifted him to his feet.

While helping him stand, she asked again, "What happened, sir?"

Mesut realized he'd forgotten everything he was going

to say as he stared blankly at the female cop who helped him get to his feet. It was as if he had swallowed all the Dutch words he knew.

Realizing he couldn't reply, she released Mesut's arm. Leaning over him, she asked again, "What happened? Can you explain please, sir? Did someone attack you? Was your house burglarized? Did you lose something? Why are you crying?"

Again, Mesut did nothing but stare in fear and astonishment. Smiling at Mesut, the female cop was taken aback when she saw bloodstains on Mesut's shirt. She sauntered to the other side of the bench without taking her eyes off Mesut.

Staring at the still wet blood, she said sternly, "If you can't speak Dutch, tell us which country you're from and we'll call you an interpreter."

Mesut's pupils bulged out and his black hair stood on end when he heard the word "translator."

While the lady cop noticed a change in him, she said, "Interpreter, interpreter, interpreter" three times consecutively. He seemed to come to his senses. Looking in the lady cop's face, he said harshly, "No!" Before the lady cop could speak, he removed a blood-covered gun as if pulling a handkerchief from his jacket pocket and placed it on the wooden counter. When the lady cop saw the gun, she was dumbfounded. The moment she got over her initial surprise, she pushed the gun away from her, leapt over the counter, twisting both of Mesut's arms and clasping them above his waist. She pushed him as far as the door she had just come from.

And after harshly swinging the door open, she said sternly, "Get in there."

Shoving Mesut inside, the female cop ordered one of her colleagues inside to bring the gun on the counter. While her colleague went out to fetch it, she escorted Mesut to a large table. She briefly explained the circumstances to a middle-aged officer sitting on the other side of the table; his hair was falling out, his nose was a little long, and his cheeks drooped slightly. The middle-aged officer jumped up when he heard the word "gun".

He came over to them, asking Mesut, "Which country did you come from?"

Mesut replied, "From Turkey." His neck was bent in submission. He felt his legs tremble again and his stature shorten. Whenever this happened, he'd cry like a child. He bit his lips to keep from crying. When the middle-aged policeman saw that Mesut was shaking and was about to cry, he had him sit in one of the chairs in front of the table and told the lady cop to bring a coffee.

She ran out and brought back a cup of coffee. Mesut took the styrofoam cup full of hot coffee in both palms. The warmth of the coffee spread from his hands to his entire body. He took two quick sips as his nerves relaxed a little.

After two more sips in a row, he began to explain without anyone asking him anything:

I've been here for 14 years. I was working in the garden. I worked for eight years without taking leave even once. I travelled to my hometown in Turkey six years ago. I got engaged to Yeli. She was the most beautiful girl in that village. We were engaged for a year. When I went on leave the following year, I organized a legendary wedding. I took Yeli and brought her here 15 days after the wedding. At first, we didn't say any harsh words to each other. I injured my back towards the spring the year I brought her here. I was walking hunched over like a senior citizen. When I was bedridden at home for a long time, I started fighting with my wife because of my frustration of being unable to do anything. Our arguing got worse over time. I beat Yeli several times. She ran away from home after one of those beatings and took refuge with one of our relatives. That relative interceded and we made up. When we went on vacation that year, I told my father-in-law that she'd run away from home. My father-in-law then proceeded to beat the living hell out of her in front of me. He scolded his daughter, "Even if your husband cuts your flesh, don't you dare make a sound. No matter what happens, your place is beside your husband!" The good old days came back when we returned from our vacation. She was doing everything I asked of her. That year, I went back to work, too, and we spent some very good times together. I worked hard and saved money for the sake of those beautiful days. I also eagerly bought a nice car.

When I told Yeli, "Get ready, we're going on vacation," she said, "you go, I'm not going on vacation." I insisted. Again, she said, "I'm not coming."

We had a serious argument and I ended up beating her again. She ran away from home again that day. I thought she went to one of her relatives again. I waited a day, a week, a month but she still hadn't returned.

The woman took refuge in one of the shelters. I learned that exactly three years later when she received her residence permit. I was really pissed off now. For those three years, I always thought about her righteousness. I put relatives in between us and we made up. I promised her I would do whatever she said. But after a while, she said, "Mesut, as you can see, instead of living like two broken-hearted people who've got nothing left of our first love, we'd better split up."

I thought she was right. That's because we were drifting away from each other day by day. I accepted her request to separate and we broke up.

After a while, I heard that she got married. The getting divorced part didn't get me down, it was her getting married to someone else and dirtying my honor that bummed me out. I thought of killing her on the spot, but one day I gave up the idea, thinking, "it's *just not worth going to jail for."* Then I deleted whatever feelings remained of her from my heart. She'd built a new life for herself and I went back to my old lonely life, too.

This summer, I went on vacation. One day, I ran into Yeli's father. He told me, *"Clean up our honor, how can you let your wife walk out on you that way? If you don't clean up our honor by next year, I'll throw your dowry in your face,"* then got up and walked away.

I ran and caught up with him. I told him I didn't want any dowry money back, but he wasn't having any of it. After putting some distance between himself and I, he turned around and yelled out, *"You've really gotten used to your foreign lifestyle, so just don't infect us with your dishonesty by talking like that."*

That hit me like a sucker punch. I wandered around the village for days like a chicken with its head cut off. I hadn't decided what to do, when one day, Yeli's mother came around and said, *"She's destroyed your heart as well as ours, and has defiled our honor. Her blood is halal for you."*

As it was, my father kept bugging me every evening, *"Am I always going to wander around the village with my head down like this?"*

Only my mother spoke on my side, saying, *"Do whatever you wish, son."*

When I returned from my summer holiday, I saw that both my relatives and acquaintances here had turned their backs on me, changing their paths whenever they spotted me. None of them wanted to have anything to do with me. By doing so, they made me feel ashamed of myself. I couldn't even turn my back on my friends with whom I confronted every day. I was afraid they would say, "The pimp couldn't keep his wife" whenever I turned my back. I couldn't sleep at night in these screwed-up circumstances.

I worked for days without any sleep. When my nerves got slack, I realized that I couldn't go on like this, so I quit my job. I played cards in the mornings in the coffeehouse and thought of Yeli in the evenings at home. But I didn't know where she was either. I searched high and low for her for about a month only to learn that they were living in our neighborhood. If only they had gone to another city, but that wasn't the case.

After keeping her husband under surveillance for a few days, I learned where they were staying. Her husband always went to work at the same time in the morning. I watched Yeli go to the corner store a few times. She had become even more beautiful. I was dying to talk to her, but at the same time, I figured she'd totally screwed me over. I was planning to kill her every night until morning, but every morning I changed my mind.

Just when I'd given up on killing her, my mother phoned last night. Her voice was tearful. It was evident from my mother's sighs that my father was forcing her. My mother's tearful voice was saying, "Son, your father says, "If he doesn't cleanse our honor, I'll disown him." Even if my father didn't disown me, she would have, but it was very tough for my mother to say, "I'll disown you, too."

I couldn't sleep until morning. As soon as morning fell, I went out and onto her street. I hid in a stairwell near their house, waiting for her husband to go to work. When her husband got in his car and left, I went and rang the doorbell. Thinking her husband had forgotten something, Yeli opened the door, and that's when I ducked inside. I held my pistol to her temple. When I got to their bedroom, I leaned my back against the wall. I pointed my gun at her forehead. We made eye contact. Her grayish-blue eyes were still sleepy. She bent her neck down. "Don't do it," she said in a dry, fearful voice. My hands started to shake. I pulled the trigger out of fear when I realized that I was freaking out. I fired two shots right in the middle of her forehead. One for my honor. And one for···

Switchblade Time

After returning from the cemetery, the bitterness and that terrible void inside me grew wider. I felt like I was falling into a deep abyss. Oddly enough, the chasm got deeper as I fell, and the deeper it got, the more terrifying it was. I was conscious as I fell, and I knew that if this dark void would come to an end, if I hit the floor, I'd shatter into a zillion pieces, but I also wanted this terrible fall that turned me inside out to end. During that fall, for a moment, I had the feeling I was dreaming with my eyes wide open. To make sure I wasn't dreaming, I got up and started walking around the house. I touched the walls, and moved some items. No, I wasn't dreaming. But I kept falling while I walked. Moreover, as I walked along, I was falling faster into that dark void. It occurred to me to hold onto someone or something or sit down. I stretched my hand out to those sitting near me. My friends, who have never left my side since the cemetery, first looked at my hand, then one of them reached out and took my hand. When I saw his hand holding my hand, I pulled back my hand in fear, but he didn't let go. Your friend's hand was one of the two hands we had just buried in the ground. He was gone, but somehow he had left one of his hands here. I was even more surprised when I looked at the other friends in the room with stunned looks. Whoever I looked at, I saw a piece of him. That meant he divided parts of himself among those who were here before he died. One of his pale lips, one of his dull and weak eyes, one of his disheveled hair, one of his long, muscleless fingers… As if it wasn't enough that I had been carrying his deficient, infirm body from place to place for years, now I had to live with his pieces. As I attempt to gather my wits, I can hear myself through my thick fleshy lips, thirsty for love and making love, I said, "No way!"

My little girl hugged my neck, asking, "What did you say, mom."

While shaking my head to mean, "I didn't say anything," a light hit the floor of the deep space I was falling into. Soaring like an eagle with huge wings, I landed smack dab in the middle of that light. In the middle of a round stage light, a primitive stage actor who shields his eyes with his hand and looks afar, was looking around with amazement, while the faces of the people in the room we were sitting in became their own faces, and the furniture in the room settled back into their original places.

As his illness worsened, he began to express about a week ago that he was going to die. He even told the time and day this was going to happen. In addition, his gaze, which sometimes turned away from himself, was always walking around the house with me, and when his lips were going somewhere, was smiling like before he said goodbye. But there was something that separated his last smile from his farewell smile. It's something diabolical and provocative. Sometimes I'd smile like him and want to get undressed in a hurry and get into bed. When my hysterical ambition passed, my hands and feet went cold and I collapsed where I was in despair. But especially when I remembered his coughing fits that came at night, I felt sorry for him and thought that I had no right to such a thing. While I was trying to overcome my pity by blaming him, for some reason I got greedy and wanted to approach him with my rude, lustful steps and shout in his face, "What the heck, he'll be checking out, while we have more good days to live."

From the day we brought him home from the hospital until he died, we used to witness the kids waking up in the morning. When the kids went to school, his gaze would wander with me for a while, and then he'd drift off to sleep. He didn't want anything or wake up until the children returned. Since the social allowance we received wasn't enough, I'd leave him while he slept and go clean homes for a few hours. But whatever the case, I'd come back before the kids got home. I didn't want the kids to see him drooling and remember that sight for the rest of their lives.

Our eldest daughter was just seven when we embarked with the hope of starting a new life away from our fears. Our only joy was to think that she would grow more freely around here. But when our daughter started to cry on the second day we were sent to the camp, she sensed her life would be more difficult than ours, whimpering, "If only we'd make our leaves green in the land where our roots remained."

After sitting and waiting for years like an abject object, we experienced the joy of being able to do something, to be useful on the first day we obtained our residence permits and started working together.

But it wasn't long before we realized that our joy was also trumped up, "This place isn't like it was made to be, Mustafa," I exclaimed.

Rubbing his aching leg, he replied, "You're right, Fatma, when I can't understand some of what they said, I can see from their looks that they don't even consider me a human being. When in fact, they don't understand what we're talking about. Sometimes I wish we could've overcome our fears and not come here. Oh, I know what I would do if I didn't have these leg pains… But I'm afraid I'll be bedridden again…" then he fell silent. That silence was to continue until he passed away.

It was the second year of our marriage. As soon as the schools were out for the summer, we went to a town in the Aegean region without telling anyone. Our elder daughter had just started kicking my stomach. At that time, no one knew anything about the motel business. It was very difficult to even find a hostel, let alone a hotel. After much searching, we were able to rent one of the two rooms from an elderly woman who lived alone. We would leave the house after breakfast in the morning and return home late in the evening. The town had a long beach covered with golden sand. But almost nobody would swim on that beach. Even though a few families of civil officials appeared towards the evening, they'd also go away after taking a brief dip in the sea, as if they were fleeing from something. On the other hand, the town locals were choosing secluded places to swim as if they were ashamed of each other, viewing the sandy golden strip like a foreigner who had invaded their land.

In the first few days, that insensitivity relaxed us, but in the following days it started to get depressing.

Sitting in the old woman's little garden after dinner, I remarked, "Mustafa, I'm bored here." The whites of his large eyes grew larger as he looked at me in the moonlight.

After tugging on his mustache, which looked like the symbol of his face and looked like a thick brush, he replied, "I'm bored too, but there's nowhere else to go. We'll go to Izmir in a day or two. The fair will open. We'll stay there for a while and come back.

"And after looking at trees for a while, what strange creatures humans are; they miss the noise in silence, as well as the crowd, the noise and the silence in the crowd. I used to think that the people living on the beaches were more alive and different than the people of our region, but after coming here, I saw with my own eyes that the reality was not like that. I wish people knew how to be happy where they are··· After a silence of deeper and deeper meaning, people are people everywhere, never mind Fatma, there's no point in thinking too much or doing philosophy. Let's make a little happiness out of this silence. Let's try to be happy by thinking there are creatures other than us living in the mountains behind the hills, fairies and gazelles are drinking water in those mountains, and gods and goddesses are having steamy sex away from human eyes. Let's forget about unhappiness by mingling with nature, whispering to us that it renews itself with the seasons. Let's pray for the health of our guest in his stomach. Also···"

He didn't finish his sentence. After that day, I couldn't get my answer whenever I tried to ask after that "also···" Or else, he just changed the direction of the conversation and glossed over my question. When he died, I thought that I'd never learn the end of that "Also···"

Yesterday, while I was making the bed that I hadn't touched for days as a memory from him, I reached out and took the pillow in my hand. I was surprised to see the notebook he kept under his pillow. How did he hide it without ever showing it to me? Why didn't he show me? At first, I thought about these things, but after a while, it hit me. Just like the light falling into that deep void. I compared myself to that primitive stage actress who looks at everything but can't even see the audience that fills the theater. With that analogy, I got rid of my dreams and entered the tunnel of life that continues again. When I took the notebook in my hand, I realized I'd learn both before and after that "Also···" The page on which he wrote his last entry was open. I started from there⋯

05.11.1984

⋯we should also go beyond ourselves, accept that Man is a lonely being, and think that we'll eventually fall into our own loneliness. That's all. The important thing is to be able to walk together as long as we can walk without falling into that loneliness (⋯)."

There are no final letters. Maybe all the strength of his sickly tired muscles was enough to get there. Maybe he couldn't keep his word and didn't write "we" because he thought it would leave me alone in the middle of nowhere.

18.10.1984

The last tremor scared me a lot. It hurts the fear of death to think that my arms, like my legs, will slowly leave me. They've been my everything for a long time.

13. 08.1984

It's a hot summer day. Fatma took me in her arms and took me outside. I was able to sit on the mat for a while with the help of my arms. Then I leaned back on the pillow. Our little girl, Sülün, went to her friend's house. She returned with a beet red face. Thinking that she was sick, Fatma and I were both scared. Turns out the girl turned red from running too much. Anyways, she got better after some rest, *and the dimples on her dark cheeks are hollow again. She hugged my neck first, then her mother's. We both relaxed when she went over to her sister. I don't know why I was so scared, but with that fear, I learned that there's one that's greater than any other fear.*

15.07.1984

They said a last check at the hospital. After that, there was nothing they could do for me. The reason for the old pains in my back are due to the weakening of my body and they'll become more and more severe. Maybe I could've been permanently paralyzed. Then I might not be able to control my arms either. Those pains started the day they threw me out of the grave with my arms tied in those cruel days of September.

08.06.1984

The unbearable pain in my legs hits my brain, I often pass out. Sometimes it feels like my back is breaking. Today, after such a painful seizure, I told Fatma to turn on the tape player. He didn't break my heart. After putting a cassette to play, she went to work. The music that spread throughout the room penetrated me. When the first tune was finished, a new tune started. Like the first song, that tune was sad as well.

> *I have a trunk made of thread and wire*
> *I have two babies made of red roses*
> *How can I leave the rose-faced love*
> *You want it like this, crazy heart,*
> *Whether you cry or laugh, crazy heart.*
> *(............(............*
>
> *years years bad years*
> *treacherous years to come.*

While listening, I thought that this song was composed for me. When in fact, I thought I'd left those bad years back in the homeland and came here, but it turns out they accompanied me.

22.02.1984

The doctor seemed to sense something sinister as he examined me. He said nothing to Fatma or I, but his increasingly tense, deepening facial features gave away his anxiety. I spoke with all the words I knew to get him to talk, but he didn't let on. He just said he'd do some research.

04.10.1983

For the first time today, I couldn't bear my aching pains. I hope this pain doesn't keep me in bed. Today was an excruciating pain that I'd never known before. It was a frightening, deathlike pain. It was also a painful, thought-provoking pain.

07.09.1983

We came to this big city exactly a year ago. In the early days, both Fatma and I thought this city would swallow us whole. We both looked like we were about to cry when we received our appointment orders. Because what we heard about this huge city up until then scared us a lot. We thought our salaries would run out as soon as we entered this city or on the first day of the month. Maybe that was our real fear. We thought that even the air we were going to buy was worth the money, but it turned out that it wasn't. The dimension of living and thinking in this city was as large as itself. You know, they say, "If you're going to drown, drown in big water." They were so right. Everything we did in the small towns we lived in could be considered a crime, and even a corporal could decide to arrest us. But here, neither the corporal takes people away, nor what is said is considered a crime. I recently attended a meeting in Aksaray. The men got up onto the podium and began shouting their heads off. Fear took me in instead of them. Now they're going to come and take us all away, I thought. I wanted to get out and get away from that fear. If I weren't ashamed of the friends I went with, I would've come home right away. I couldn't leave, but for a long time, my gaze was fixed on the door. But no one came, nor did they take us from there. Had they been there, we would've submitted ourselves thinking they'd come and take us all away after these conversations. It's nothing like our little hellish town; it hides both the good and the bad.

01.08.1982

Everything is hidden under the wings of fear. We even avert our eyes from each other. Inside and out.

30.06.1982

Everything and everyone is becoming increasingly more alien to each other.

27.05.1982

Those who relate this history to me will have misunderstood. I wonder how those days were different from these days of fear we live in? Wasn't that blow similar to this blow? Some friends say, "They emptied this history," but to me, there was nothing in it anyway. Or it was just as painful as it is today. The ones I have left from the fact this history is updated every year, and those who have me write the annual balance sheet, saying, "summer is beautiful," didn't even bother to show it to me this year. In case I might add something objectionable to their notes···

01.05.1982

Five years ago, they smeared blood on the Eid in Istanbul in preparation.

23 Nisan 1982

I'm in no mood to think about the past or the future. It's as if my body was going to betray me. One day the muscles on one side of me twitch, while those on my other side twitch another day.

10.04.1982

I can't explain to my children the reason for the twitch or the bruises on my body, I try not to show the blood mixed with my saliva even to my wife.

03.04.1982

After throwing me on the concrete like a rag, the man said, "If you come across me again, then I will break your bones that I couldn't break now." It's like I'm willingly confronting you. I wonder, what did he mean? Or am I a goner from here?

07.03.1982

As soon as we walked in, they started hitting, saying, "You had a nice, relaxing two days in our hotel." I was ashamed of myself when they put the club against my anus, but they weren't ashamed of what they had done. They keep saying, "talk." I wish I had something to talk about. Then what do I care that someone else killed them?

05.03.1982

I'm here for the third time. Even the walls are starting to look familiar now. When my eyes get used to the dark, I take out my notebook and write. Even though I can't get out of here myself, my shoes must be taken off. They haven't touched my notebook for the second time. I guess they either don't really see it or else they know something.

01.01.1982

I can't believe how much cruelty fits a year!

17.10.1981

They arrested the sociology teacher with her sociology book. We teach, but we don't learn from anything.

16.06.1981

It's the second time Fatma, our daughter and I are going on vacation. I'm in a joyful mood as we'll be away from here for awhile, and I'll see new faces. We had a very tough winter, so I think it will be good for all of us to get away from here.

20.02.1981

Every time they come around, they search our house, they can't find anything, but they're still looking. What's their purpose for such scrutiny?

26.01.1981

For the second time, we saved our asses. If the bruises on my body go away, I think I'll forget everything. But I can't get rid of the pain in my lower back that started after I was hit.

11.01.1981

I never thought of these places while drinking raki with friends 10 days ago. For the first time, I was consoled that they were intimidating. But the fellows just follow it every day. They took the toothpick left in my pocket, why didn't they touch my notebook and pen?

14.01.1980

They brought us all from school. They released our friends who aren't from here in one day. Only I remained. Nothing's registered···

13.09.1980

If it goes on like this, nothing or nobody will be remaining here.

12.09.1980

A silence has descended everywhere.

01.07.1980

We decided to go on vacation with Fatma.

24.06.1980

We got married yesterday.

04.04.1980

I bought this notebook to commemorate my fifth year of teaching. I'm going to keep a diary from now on. Maybe not daily, but I'll write as much as I can. (⋯.)

Snowy Images

There was a guy named Riza. A smile was never missing from his plump red lips. His pupils were like two dark moles moving in a white sea. As he didn't like to be alone, he always looked over his shoulder at others, whether he was working or walking. While, age-wise, he was the runt of his class, his burly body rivaled those two years older. Although no one especially fed him, his hands were still meaty, swollen and fluffy like dough in the oven. He always felt he was wobbling like a huge top while walking. The spin of that top would accelerate especially even more when he ran, and he'd scare the wits out of people because he was on the verge of toppling over.

The arid, harsh cold of autumn suddenly subsided exactly a month and a half after I started working in that village, and the soft, deceptive cold of winter set in. I didn't mind at all when it first snowed, because I'd been used to it since I was small. However, in the coastal city of the Black Sea, where I went to study in recent years, the snow wouldn't stick where it fell like in our hometown, it would melt after two days. Oddly enough, I was used to this last situation and I didn't mind, thinking that the snow falling in the village would melt away in two days. But just as that first snow didn't vaporize, the snowfall that started two days later continued for days. Until then, I had never seen such relaxing snow falling. Even though the snow was falling lackadaisically and getting a little thicker by the day, I was thinking optimistically that the snow would melt once it stopped falling. Although it was a bit difficult for me to accept, after a while I gave up hope for the snow to melt. I wouldn't be able to take a pleasant walk around the neighborhood after classes, and I wouldn't be able to sit under the moonlight until late. I acknowledged this, but I'd get very depressed when I thought of the long winter nights I'd spend alone. At one point I thought that every snowflake was falling to enslave me into those long nights. But I was relieved when the pure white truth covered the mountains like a cotton bird's wing. I felt compelled to find new hobbies to forget my troubles. The first thought that came to mind was to measure the thickness of the snow. I made a snow-measuring tool by dividing a two-meter long straight stick into centimeters and millimeters. On days when it was snowing, I'd regularly look at my measuring instrument morning and evening, and write down the thickness of the snow in a notebook. After I recorded it, I was comparing it to a week ago and speculating on how thick the snow would be a week later if it fell like this. I quit this job, which I'd been conducting earnestly for months, in the evening when I felt like a lonely person who had fallen onto the other side of the world. The reason I quit was because the last man in the village had traveled to Istanbul two days after New Year's. He was the only person I could talk to. When he was gone, the only thing I could talk to in the evenings was the cold, implacable blizzard outside. As soon as it got dark, it turned into a huge cave of silence, and neither the misty mountains visible from my window from time to time nor the white-clad pine trees on the mountain peaks could console me. While I was struggling with my solitude like this, Rıza and the other kids would walk to school every morning trampling through the snow every which way, and when school let out, they'd return home the way they had come. Since the mothers had their children wear tight boots, their socks didn't get very wet, but since Rıza didn't have a mother, his socks were always wet when he arrived at school. This was partly due to the fact that he wobbled like a spinning top. But he didn't care he was wet or cold. Maybe he considered himself the happiest child in the world because he came to school like the others. Rıza would have no clothes that didn't get wet. But Riza was very happy to come to school.

Everyone in the village knew the story of Rıza's father and mother down to the smallest detail. Before the men went abroad to work, I'd listen to their stories first in any house I went to. But what surprised me was that almost everyone told the story in the same words and in the same way. In fact, no matter who spoke, their facial features were approximately the same depth. Anyone begins to tell their story, after saying that they loved each other very much and that Rıza's mother Zarife left her first husband for Rıza's father Hasan, "Zarife was going to give birth to her sixth child. She didn't tell anyone her birthday was coming, probably because she was ashamed. She just said to Hasan, "I'm not in the mood today." But after taking a deep breath, "Hasan, look, we'll have another mouth to feed. Don't even think of leaving your job for me, take the children and go to the field. I'm not in the mood but I don't think anything will happen today. If anything happens, I'll send you news with someone," she said. When she said that, Hasan took the children and went to the field. It was as if her labor pains were waiting for Hasan and the children to leave. They had just left the village when Zarife's labor pains began. She must've considered severing her own child's umbilical cord, as she never informed anyone. It was a long time before the old folks in the village heard Zarife's screams. The old folks all gathered around her, but no matter what they did, they could not stench the bleeding. They brought news to Hasan with the fastest walkers, but they were too late. There was nary a drop of blood remaining in Zarife's veins when Hasan arrived. Seeing her lying so lifeless, Hasan's cries never stopped. After interning her in the cemetery, they couldn't pry him away from her gravesite for four days and four nights. When his crying turned into a weird moaning, he got up and went into the forest. He only replied to those who went to bring him back, "I don't deserve to live after my Zarife," and said that he wouldn't go back until he died. Those who followed him got fed up, but not him. He added his voice to the sound of the raging brook, as he sang mournful dirges in the forest. Some nights he came around and monologued at Zarife's graveside.

When the seasons changed and the weather got chilly, he suddenly remembered he had other children who remained in his custody from Zarife. Returning home, he said, "I couldn't die with the dead, at least I'll find some solace dealing with those remaining in her memory." When he saw that the harvest gathered by the children was too little to survive the winter, Hasan became anxious. He decided to buy wheat to complete the winter flour. After saying one more time at Zarife's grave - "I'll be with you soon" - he got on a truck that was coming to buy salt for the salt cellar. Kamyo crossed the mountains and started on a straight road. It left Zara and started to travel towards Kanlı Sivas. Was it the driver's carelessness or brake failure, we'll never know, but the truck couldn't maneuver through a turn and jackknifed into a roadside ditch. The truck flipped over at a high rate of speed. Of the five or six people sitting on the truck bed when the accident occurred, Hasan was the only one who was squashed beneath the overturned truck.

It was the snowy winter of that year Zarife and Hasan died and Rıza was orphaned. As if January's whistling blizzards weren't enough, bitter cold would set in whenever they ceased. It was more of a chill than cold. One didn't want to go outside for fear of "I'm going to freeze immediately."

One day, when the horrific cold prevailed, the wind picked up the fresh snow that fell at night and dumped it on the paths of the children. When I looked out the window in the morning, the snowfall and cold winds continued to blow the snow to and fro. I thought the children wouldn't come to school that day. But I still got up at the usual time. My room was freezing. I tossed some dry firewood I had prepared the previous evening. I then ignited the kindling and placed it on top of the wood in the stove. I filled the big teapot with water and put it on the stove. As I ran into bed and waited for my room to warm up, I began to listen to the crackling sounds of the burning kindling. I got up and looked out the window. Despite the snowfall, the sun attempted to make an appearance in the distance. Seeing that false sun, I remembered that the children had come to school in worse weather before. I grabbed my coat and ran to the classroom next door. Again, I ignited the wood in the large-sized steel stove, which I prepared the night before. I didn't have much hope for the children's future, but I still lit the stove. My room was toasty warm with the burning kindling. The water in the teapot was on the verge of boiling. I prepared my breakfast while the tea brewed. After doing my morning cleaning and drying my hands and face, I brewed my tea. I had eaten two or three bites, half-dressed, when I saw children passing by the window one by one. Something happened in my body that I had never felt before. I thought my heart would break and the hairs on my skin would grow out of their own accord. For a while, I closed my eyes and listened to the footsteps of the children tramping into the classroom. I quickly ate my breakfast and got dressed. I took the tea in the teapot and a few glasses from the cupboard and went to class. I first gave cups of tea to the little ones from the far village. I wanted to give it to the elder ones, but they didn't want any.

The lesson began. Since the five classes were together, I was teaching in level groups. I assigned homework to the elders and those who knew better, then dealt with the middle group. The first graders were lingering and waiting for me. When the group in the middle turned in the homework, it was their turn. Though they were few in number, I needed to deal mostly with them. In addition, Rıza wanted constant attention with the gaze of his black eyes like a darting flame. I was tired of dealing with them. I also had to check the seniors' homework. I directed the little ones to write, then sat in my chair. While checking the homework of those who had finished, I felt something bugging me deep down inside. First, I looked at Rıza's socks, which were spread on the wood next to the burning stove with steam piping out of them, and then at the window. I thought that both the mountains visible in the distance and the falling snow were planning to imprison me within the walls. I was trying to overcome my boredom by leaning my back against my chair back and gazing blankly out the window again. But Riza wasn't leaving me alone. He came up to me after every sentence he wrote. Then after every word he wrote. Finally, he began coming up to me after every letter she wrote. He was obviously starved for attention, but I also wanted to listen to myself a little bit.

The last time he came up to me, I admonished him, "Go away!"

After instinctively taking a few steps back towards his desk, Riza halted in his tracks and turned slightly towards me. He looked at his notebook in one hand, then back at me. Then he turned to look at his steaming socks. He turned to me again, as he bit his meaty lower lip lightly with his upper teeth.

Turning his whirring eyes towards the floor, embarrassed, he bowed his head a little and asked weakly, "Where shall I go?"

The Girl with the Silver Voice

Having not seen the sun for months, my body was ecstatic when it saw it shining brightly in the endless blue sky. I was lying on the warm sand in the tranquility of my slackened muscles. Even though I'd lift my head from time to time to watch the rippling blue waters, I was constantly dismissing the dreams and fantasies that were invading my mind so that I might savor the moment. While I was dealing with my inner ordeals, I heard a suave female voice coming from nearby. The sound seemed not to come from a human throat, but from a tuned musical instrument.

While I turned on my side to look in the direction of the sound, the woman's voice repeated the same word in the same way, "Ayala···"

There is something inexplicable about a catchy melody. It's like magic that overwhelms the emotions as it aims for the heart. When I heard the sound for the third time, I forgot myself and turned my head hastily to look in the direction of the sound. Dozens of holiday makers lying side by side must've also wondered about the sound because they were peering in the direction I was looking. It was hard to tell to whom the voice belonged. I sat helplessly, waiting for it to resonate.

Before long, I could hear it again, this time, with a little tremolo and twice consecutively, "Ayala, Ayala,"

The owner of the voice was a middle-aged woman, not far from me, whose hips looked as if they were protruding from her thighs. Shielding her eyes against the sun with her hands, she was gazing at the blue sea while repeating the same word in her soft voice. She had tiny breasts that didn't match her large bony body and long legs. Besides, nobody would've ever thought the owner of this steamy, emotional and stimulating voice could be that woman.

While I was thinking about how nature made this disproportion, I started comparing our bodies. I had a slightly dark complexion, while she had pale skin. In contrast to my chubby short legs, she had long, lean legs. Our breasts were also inversely proportional, my breasts strikingly large and erect, hers too small and flabby to suit her body. Her eyes were light blue, mine were pitch black. The only similar part of our body was our hair. Both our hairs were straight, black, and cropped short. But her black hair added a special feature to her white skin, while my hair blended into my tan body and disappeared.

This time, after the woman lowered her hands, which she had used to shield her eyes from the sun, she said, "Ayalaaa," elongating it.

Now her voice added a tone that was very difficult to reach. The short intermittent rhythm of her voice upturned all my senses. I couldn't understand how this happened, it was as if the woman's voice was touching my skin like a hand. Not only that, but her tone went further and touched my fantasies. I was suddenly overcome by a crazy feeling. I looked around desperately, thinking of getting up and going over to the woman. My face reddened as if others understood my mixed emotions.

I lay on my back on the warm sand to forget everything and enjoy the sun again, when a voice softer than the woman's voice from very close to me said, "Mommy."

With the haste of a harpooned fish, I leapt up and sat down. I looked in the direction from where the voice came. This time, the owner of the voice was a young girl who'd just emerged from the sea and with clear water droplets running down her skin. She tossed her auburn straight hair back with a nod, then looked at her mother, who'd just called her. She didn't look like her mother at all. She must've seen me leaping up from where I was lying and sitting down, because she glanced at me with a brief look in which she fit a smile. She had neither her mother's large protruding bones nor long legs. Her overall body proportions matched the two blue eyes that adorned her round, white face. But strangely enough, I recognized this girl with the silver voice. And I've known her for years. I always wanted to see her, but I could never see her. She stood before me now, both with her silver voice and her walk that I'd imagined for years.

I couldn't make out the mother and daughter's conversation, but I listened to their emotional voices. After conversing for a while, they got up and walked towards the hotel together.

The silver-voiced girl's gliding gait beside her mother was very similar to that of ballerinas traipsing onto stage. Maybe she was a ballerina at the Bolshoi. Maybe she also played in the Swan Lake Ballet. It would be nice to see her gliding like a swan on stage. While she was floating like that in her white tutu clinging to her long arms, broad shoulders and slim waist···

I don't know why, but as they started walking towards the hotel, I hurriedly followed behind. But they disappeared in the blink of an eye by the time I entered the lobby. I ran into the entrance hall, looked at the elevator and down the corridors of each floor. I went up and down in the elevator many times, but I couldn't see them anywhere. Desperate, I returned to the seaside again.

I waited for them by taking an occasional dip in the sea until sundown. But they didn't return. Moreover, while I was looking for them, the inflatable blue lilo on which the girl lay in the sea had also disappeared. Maybe I'd never see it again. I went into a funk with just the thought I'd never see her again. Disgusted with myself, I gathered up my stuff and walked up towards my hotel room. After hanging out in the room for a while, I took a shower and dried off. Before going down to dinner, I went out to the balcony to put on some make-up and chill out a bit. I thought I'd take a look around down below before I took a seat. I looked down and noticed dinner had begun. By the wide window of the restaurant, mother and daughter were sitting side by side, chatting while they dined. I quickly combed my wet hair and left my room.

As soon as I got my food, I started looking for a table to sit at. Of all the empty tables, I went over and sat at the table next to theirs. My face was turned towards them. I wanted to see their faces and hear their voices. I didn't know whether I wanted to hear Ayala's or her mother's voice. But I did want to hear their voices as they spoke. Ayala spoke with her blue eyes squinting. The white daisies on her light blue blouse practically waived as she spoke. Her other movements, such as her gait and silver voice, were full of dance. For a while, I put down my fork and knife and just stared at them naively. The big-boned woman, who the silver-voiced girl often called "Mommy", lightly caressed my eyes when she saw me looking at them. A vibration shook my body as she took a huge bite and buried it between her lips.

As I started to eat my food again, I asked myself, "What is it about these women's voices that strikes me?" I didn't have an answer. So, how did I know this girl? Could I have seen her before and where? Seeing the increasing number of questions in my mind, I decided to invite them for a cup of after-dinner coffee and a chat. When I made my decision, I was filled with an incomprehensible tranquility.

Smiling to myself, I muttered, "They probably know as much English as my broken English."

But suddenly, while the sentence, "What if they don't know?" upset me a little, the bitterness it created soon passed. Without losing my initial optimism, I consoled myself once again, saying, "They know as much as I do. That's enough for us to get along."

While I was eating my dinner and looking around, I recalled all the low earning workers at the hotel, from the waiter to the cook, were Bulgarian immigrants, a thin sad smile crossed my lips again, muttering, "They've got cheap workers here, we're beyond···"

But such clarity of mind, my ability to fathom everything together took me to the table of the two women again. As I looked at them, I said in a whistling voice, "If we can't understand each other in one language, I'll call over one of those immigrants and ask my questions,,,"

While I was trying to finish my meal, I kept them under surveillance. Suddenly, the books I read from Russian literature began passing before my eyes, as if in a parade. Why did the heroines in most of them remain indelibly stamped in my mind? I always thought of them as they were in those pages. They all had an impression of being cold and distant from me. All were like that but one. Nevertheless, I couldn't figure out which one it was.

I strained my mind a little but to no avail. But how did

The Girl with the Silver Voice

I know this girl whose mother calls Ayala and whom I call Silver Voice? I've seen her, but I can't remember where. At best, she must've been one of those gymnasts who jumped and swung around like they were rubber Gumby toys. I don't know anyone else besides them. Although I peered far into the depths of my mind, I couldn't discern where I knew her. I was about to finally decide that I didn't know her from anywhere when the silver-voiced Ayala looked at me and smiled.

All I could say for her mother was that she resembled a powerful old horse, but the silver-voiced Ayala was like a slender colt running after it and springing up on its hind legs. Even the way she swept her hair back was like the way a colt swung its mane. Also, her mother was trying to stand upright with her big bones and look strong, but in my opinion, her weak side was more dominant. I didn't know why I had such a feeling when I looked at the woman, but my intuition was telling me this by whistling. Regardless what her mother was, why was this girl's clear and soft voice, which I compare to silver, affecting me so much? It was like a voice I had heard before. But I couldn't figure it out where I'd heard it before. Just as I started to search for an answer to this question, Ayala's mother left her alone and hurriedly headed towards the information desk and then started ascending the stairs opposite the desk. At first, I was a little anxious that Ayala would also get up and leave but when I saw the girl sitting calmly and looking beyond the sea, I was relieved. Her shoulders lifted slightly as she placed her elbows on the table. Her already thin waist seemed to get a little thinner with this pose. But the widening of her shoulders was telling me a lot. I thought she had thrown a shawl over her now bare shoulders. There was no such recollection in my memory. At this stage, the character that suited her best was ballerina. She was a ballerina and I had seen her on at most one TV show. If I hadn't seen her, I had seen a ballerina who was a splitting image of her. I didn't know the time, but it was definitely like that. Otherwise, how could I know someone I've seen for the first time in my life and will never see again from now on? The only possibility was that she was a member of the Bolshoi crew. If she were a gymnast, I could've seen at least one muscle stiffen by now. Her muscles were like her soft voice from the beach until now.

By the time her mother came back, she'd already eaten her fruit. Her mother had a bag in each of her shovel-like hands. She placed the smaller one in front of the girl. After glancing at the people eating at the other tables, the girl took her make-up out of her bag and applied it carelessly. When she was done, she looked into her mother's eyes. Her mother glanced at the tiny watch on her wrist, turning her eyes that seemed as if they were about to pop over the top of her freckled face.

As soon as she had looked at the time, she hurriedly stood up and said to her daughter, "C'mon, we're going," as she headed back towards the information desk.

Ayala began staggering after her. I was surprised at what was happening. I muttered to myself, "At least I'll take these plates of mine to where the empties are put so I can fall in behind them," as I got up hastily.

As soon as I had left them on the dirty dishes table, I sauntered in the direction they were going. They were transiting the space in front of the information desk towards the glazed outer door. The silver-voiced footsteps grew even more timid. It was as if she didn't feel like walking behind her mother. I sped up a little to catch up with them. They picked up the pace too, as if they realized that I had sped up. I looked around and started running when the big-boned woman pushed open the glass door. Ayala glided out through the opening door. Her mother followed behind her, leaving the door unchecked. While I paused so the door wouldn't hit me, I saw a black car with fully tinted windows pull up in front of the hotel. Her mother glided into the back, and silver-voiced Ayala jumped in the front of the car. As the car moved off, I felt some movement in my mind. As I looked around in bewilderment, I saw Anna Karenina, flitting about in her black fur, ignoring the falling snow as she approached a waiting car.

As my mind panned between shifting images, I smiled, "Looks like not all Russian girls are Anna Karenina!"

The Fish and The Monument

The two of us, a swan and I, were near the shoreline of the lake situated north of the large park. There was a fish in the lake besides us. I was swimming, the swan was laughing, and the fish was walking. The fish swam when it got tired. I walked, while the swan watched us, its neck stretched out. When the fish in the water started acrobatics, he caused the swan to burst into fits of giggling. But his laughter was not as nice as himself. The fish didn't mind his hideous chortling either. In fact, when the swan started guffawing, the fish jumped even higher and dove into the dark waters with a few flips in the air, and then jumped back into the air from the point from where it had dived. As I watched his buffoonery, I began to seriously wonder what kind of fish he was. While I was thinking about which species it was, two streams came to my mind, with trout in one and carp in the other. Those were the two streams of my childhood. They would converge at one place and flow together, twisting and turning.

Suddenly moving away from the shore, the fish sprinted to the middle of the lake and began to continue its acrobatics there. But this time the swan wasn't laughing. I couldn't tell if he was angry at the fish's departure or if I disagreed with his laughter. He suddenly extended his neck upwards. He even belittled the flowers around him. He turned toward the fish, angry at something else, something in love. Snapping his beak as he shouted at the fish, "Don't splash around the waters and spoil my dream." He told me he couldn't find time to smile, let alone laugh, then he turned around on one foot and like a prima-donna, he said he had a dream to tell me about.

While I gave him a bewildered look, he put his other foot on the ground and began relating his dream:

I was a baby again in the dream I'd just had. My mother had caught me by the wing and was dragging me towards a cliff with her beak. We advanced as far as the edge of the cliff. My mother was still grasping my wing tightly. I was getting ready to say, "Mom, you're hurting me," when an uprooted, gnarly tree rushed past us. When it was a little far from us, flames engulfed it.

Gaping first at the tree and then at me, my mother exclaimed, "We were really lucky."

While I was trying to free my aching wing, which my mother held tightly, I yelled out, "But you were going to throw me off the cliff."

My mother looked at me and grinned. In a voice that wasn't at all similar to the one just before and that was frightening, she said, "You're wrong," but somehow she ceased to be my mother.

All of a sudden, its beak disappeared. She wore a wolf mask on her head. When I saw her like that, I was afraid of what to do. Both my legs and wings began to tremble.

A duck emerged from the tall grass on the opposite shore of the lake with hasty steps, and plunged into the water as if a horseman was chasing after him. It started swimming towards us quickly. While we were both thinking, "He's coming to listen to our conversations," he started to swim in a wide arc over the lake to where the fish were jumping.

Just as we were saying he had "set his mind to catch the fish," he made a sharp turn and started swimming towards the shore. He came ashore at a place very close to us. He ignored us and dove into the scrub on the shore. The swan stared at him angrily for a while, then continued to relate his dream from where he had left off:

When my mother leaned towards me with the wolf mask, I was scared out of my wits and fainted. After a while, I regained my senses with the hard blows of my mother's beak. No matter how hard my mother tried to make me laugh, I could only look fearful at her face with dull eyes. For some reason, her image wouldn't vacate my eyes. The weather was also very warm. But I was cold to the bone in the bed my mother put me in and my teeth were chattering. Meanwhile, my father came over to us. He touched the swelling on both sides of my throat with his hand. He said softly, "It'll pass. You'll get over it."

After waiting for a while without breathing, he handed me half the candy he took out of his pocket, saying, "You'll get better when you eat this. I had a difficult time finding it, but it'll heal you."

I looked at him with my eyes, which I forced open, and took the candy he was holding out. With his help, I put it in my mouth. My father took the other half of the candy out of his pocket and placed it under my pillow. He touched the swelling on the side nearest to him again with his fingertips.

"Whooping cough," said my mother calmly.

Looking away from us as if she was ashamed of what she said, she sat at my feet and started to cry. I could hear her voice, but I couldn't call out to her and say, "Don't cry!" because of my parched throat. My pain was increasing. In fact, I thought my flesh would fall to the ground in pieces as I breathed. That's when I had another incessant coughing fit. My weak body shook several times under the impact of the coughing. I fainted while half of the candy that my father had put under my pillow was floating around in my head.

When I came to, I felt like I had stepped out of a deep, dark abyss. As with every recycling from that death junction, the air and my mother smelled bad again after this transformation.

Two more ducks began to swim towards us, following the path of the first. At first they were both swimming calmly along the same line. But as they swam to the middle of the lake, one of them made a sudden thrust forward. The other dived under the water, looking intently after him. After a while, he surfaced next to his buddy who had passed him. They started swimming side by side again. They swam like that for a while, checking on each other, and came ashore at the spot where the first one came out. One was black and white and one was a drake. The Swan shook its head as the Ducks soon swam back as if in remorse.

Frowning angrily after them, he said, "One day, when I came back from one of those deaths, I heard my mother cry a little loudly. She no longer smelled bad. With my eyes, I wanted her to lift my arms and hug me. When she hugged me with a smile, a teardrop from her cheeks fell on my cheek for the first time. I wanted her to hug me with a smile. For some reason, I involuntarily shuddered when I felt the warmth of her tears for the first time. With that shudder, I wrapped my arms tightly around my mother's neck."

Having kept out of sight for a long time, the fish jumped up from the abyss, ignoring the ducks very close by. Cartwheeling in the air again, he plunged back into the water. The swan nodded, looking at the fish then at me.

While I looked at him, the fish came up to the surface, poked his mouth out of the water remarking, "I expected his dream to have had a happy ending when he ate candy. Now you're going to listen to my dream."

When I glanced at my watch, he shouted angrily, "You listened to him···"

Nodding, I signaled I was going to listen, whereby the fish began to tell about his dream.

I fell into a deep slumber in the shade of a plane tree overlooking the blue waters that had taken root on an islet in the middle of another lake where I went on a picnic with my mother. Suddenly, the water of the big lake started to boil. I woke up when my body started to heat up. I was trying to see what was going on around me with my sleepy eyes, when I heard an explosion. Right after the sound of the explosion, my parents' intestines burst out. Neither the sound that ruptured their intestines nor the thing that produced the sound could be seen. When I looked at them, I thought that their bellies might have ruptured on their own, as I saw they didn't even shed a drop of blood. I was floored. Forgetting that the water was boiling, I immersed my head in the water I thought the stench would snap the bridge of my nose. Regardless of the direction I turned or swam, I couldn't be rid of that awful stink. Moreover, I couldn't open my eyes. When I managed to open them, they were burning. That's when it happened. The lake suddenly rose to the sky and overflowed to the shore. It was like an invisible giant had inhaled the lake water with its breath, and then spit it out vigorously when its mouth filled. I too had risen upwards with the water of the lake. While I was way up high, an unbearably hot wind took the water and me and started tossing me into the void. When the wind left us, we fell into a field that was hotter than the sun. The water caught fire the moment it hit the ground. As soon as it freed itself of the flames, it evaporated and mixed with the heat.

As I writhed in pain as if I was in a hot frying pan, the soil said with infuriated tears, "A light just passed through here. It was warmer than any light I've ever seen. That light that burned all the living things on me. He'll make you vomit and kill you until you're out of it, too."

He looked at me and said, "Look, the depth has already started to pour off." The first duck to the shore emerged from the scrub he had just dove into and waddled over to the lakeshore. After pausing a bit, he alighted, vectoring all his strength to his wings. After drawing a rainbow over the lake, he glided down to the opposite shore.

When I saw my skin was falling out, I leapt up with fear and started running quickly. I started running, but a tsunami was coming faster from behind me. I was running and shouting. Just when the flood was about to reach me, I woke up to my own voice.

Whatever the first duck that glided down to the opposite shore was thinking, he waddled up calmly to the lakeshore again. After looking about with an inviting gaze as he lowered himself into the cool waters. Like the first duck, the other two ducks dived into the cool waters from a place where the green trees were smiling into the lake.

The tree leaves rustled under the impact of the blowing wind. The fish dove into the water and the swan flew off. When they left, I walked down the path between the trees and reached the green patch near the lake. I went over to a monument in the middle of the patch, which was erected symbolizing a peace treaty signed between the Holy Roman Empire and the Principality of Orange-Nassau of 1697. I put on my glasses and started reading the inscription etched on the monument:

D.O.M.

PACIFERO

S.

PALRYVICENSI

IN. IPSO

RIVINOSAE. AEDIS

SOLO

H.M.P.

GVILIELMVSV

NASSAV-AVRIAVS.

A.D.

CI(I) CCLXXXXII.

Funeral Preludes

I paced from one end to the other of the long, narrow living room of our house several times and took a seat in one of the light brown armchairs. I turned on the TV to get rid of the tired malaise in my eyes. A documentary on a channel caught my attention. There was something odd about the flight of a flock of birds, which the cameraman shot with all his dexterity.

The birds used their tails instead of their wings as they flew in a circle. It was obvious the cameraman used a camera trick he knew in the shoot, but it wasn't easy to fathom what was happening at first glance. That's because there was some constant change in this strange train. The only thing invariable was the bird flying in the middle. Only its flight pattern and distance from others hadn't changed at all.

After flying interminably in such a circular and continuous motion, the birds took a break on a high rock at the entrance of a lush valley. There was no change in their order during the break, either. While the people in the circle were admiring the beauty of the green valley, that bird in the middle was looking thoughtfully in front of it. Seeing his sad, melancholic state, my mind fluttered as the words 'thinking commander' spilled from my lips. While I was thinking about the reason for this trick my mind is playing on me, I muttered aloud, "Perhaps the enthusiastic soldiers stare at the shore in admiration; Both Agamemnon, Barbaros, Tariq Bin Ziyad and Lord Gürzon looked in front of me with such sadness." But for some reason, I was afraid of my own voice. To overcome my fear, I wandered around the walls of the living room and turned back to the screen. The bird in the middle spread its old feathered wings in the front.

While I was thinking they'd "alight" in my mind, the bird in the middle slowly gathered its open wings and then spoke into the middle with a voice like a scream, "Everything's at the end of this valley."

I couldn't understand the last word as he hissed in his beak.

Hearing what he said, the other birds looked ahead. Looking in front of them as if ashamed of their joy, the bird in the middle dipped its gaze into the greenery of the vast valley. His weazened eyes were filled with sadness. I was also saddened by the interaction established between us in a short time. I shuddered and got goosebumps when a screeching distress that had been boiling up inside me so quietly for days mixed with that sadness.

"It's close," I said, as if I knew it. I grimaced. I got up and began traipsing amongst the ornamental plants in flowerpots lining the walls of the tall living room. But when the sad boredom brimming inside me took over my whole body, I gave up walking around the room and headed towards the bedroom. As I opened the door to the narrow hall, my gaze fell on the TV screen again. The birds still hadn't gotten airborne. As I felt the weariness on my face, the melancholy that seemed like a scream inside me started to strain my lips. I walked to the bedroom. I looked out of the bedroom window as I muttered, "This is the best way to drown out this ringing, these noises, and this boredom···"

Unable to shake the trees, the exhausted wind gently ruffled the branches of the trees. Neither the play of the wind nor the branches teasing each other could distract me from my thoughts. Meanwhile, like a scream inside me, my sad distress got more aggravated. I hurriedly threw myself on the bed. As I pulled the blanket over my head as if the light was the cause of it all, and buried myself in the darkness, the bell of the nearby church began to ring. It was a little past noon. I thought the bell would ring a few times, but it seemingly never stopped. It was pealing as if it was inside the bedroom. I tucked my head under the pillow in order not to hear the bell. The chime sounded much less, but this time another bell sounded in my brain. My breathing constricted as the bells in my brain grew louder. I tried a few times to turn my head and breathe easier, but it didn't work.

When I felt like I was going to suffocate, I threw both the pillow and blanket off in fear and sat on the edge of the bed. But I was drenched in sweat in those few minutes of suffocation. As I combed my sweaty hair with my fingers, I felt the cry-like sadness inside my body once again spread throughout my body.

Listening to the sound of the church bell ringing at

brief intervals, I said, "Everything always starts with such a sound," and lay down on the bed again.

This time, the swinging image of the bell appeared before my eyes.

Uttering a word every time it swung to and fro, it completed its sentence, "it··· doesn't··· start··· with··· a··· sound···it··· starts···with··· my··· sound···and···ends··· with··· mine···."

After a moment of silence, as if to strike a powerful blow, it said, "it's only your moment between the beginning and the end."

After waiting for as long as a round trip, it exclaimed, "Before and after that, it's mine," and went quiet.

As my pensive eyes shone as if waking from sleep, it said in a whisper, "The moment given to you began with the hammer blow of one master will end with the hammer blow of another master."

A brown-painted coffin appeared before my eyes as I smiled as if I had taken my revenge on the bell. A coffin was borne on the shoulders of four men wearing black suits. With the coffin, the men proceeded down a corridor whose huge glass doors opened onto other halls and entered a hall with wooden doors. A man in dark blue clothes came out of another room shortly after they disappeared behind that big door; stating, "Those who want to talk, please have their names written down." While we were looking at the floor decorated with mosaics of various colors, as if searching for something, a man who was gesturing towards the door where the black-robed men had just entered with the coffin on their shoulders, saying, "C'mon in." Dressed in blue, two female attendants were accompanying us on both sides, as we walked past the large white-faced man in a navy blue dress and proceeded towards the inner halls. While the two of them held open the wings of the large wooden door on both sides, we entered the hall with its dark green armchairs. The four black-clad men weren't there, but the brown coffin they were carrying was on the black marble catafalque in the middle that looked like it was buried in the flowers around it. Shortly after we sat in the crescent-shaped chairs around the catafalque, the music of the funeral symphony emanating from all over the dimly lit hall plunged us into the mystical air inside.

As the dead silence made our bodies tremble, the music slowed down considerably. Keeping up with the slowing music, one of the attendants with blond hair, blue eyes, and blue outfit walked to the podium near the coffin. As if he wanted to extricate us from the silence in which we were buried in fear, he read the text that brought Leo in the coffin closer to us, then called Leo's wife, Suzan to the podium.

In the softest of all her voices I've ever heard, Suzan said, "Dear Leo." She caressed the coffin for a while with her gaze.

"Dear Leo," she said again, as if she'd forgotten what

she had said before. She paused for a while. With a voice that had thickened a little and choked in her throat, she said, "What can I say now, after all the nice years we spent together?" Her voice got stuck in her throat. She stood for a while doing nothing. "You knew how to spend your best time for me, for our children, and for others," she said after wiping her tears with the back of her hand, and again fell silent.

She looked at their son, whom they still called 'Leo Junior,' sitting in the front row of dark green crescent-shaped chairs. Turning towards the coffin, she said, "I never thought that such a separation could happen so quickly," and her sad voice melted away in the dimness of the hall. She turned to look at those gathered in the hall again. if telling Leo Junior, she finished her speech with, "I don't know how far we can make it, but from now on we'll try to live without you."

The speakers after that also said what they had to say. When the conversations were over, we all walked in front of the coffin in a neat line and with leisurely steps, murmuring a few broken phrases expressing our desperation in the face of death, saying farewell and leaving Leo in his coffin alone, we proceeded into the consolation hall. The music of the funeral prelude could be heard from every corner of the consolation hall, as was in the departure hall. I stood in line to offer my condolences to Suzan and Leo Junior when I heard the phone ringing in the long living room of our house.

The sound of the phone brought my dull eyes to life and I was pulled away from my thoughts waiting in line. I got out of bed and ran towards our living room. I looked at the TV while holding the receiver to my ear. The birds were getting ready to alight. As I thought to myself, "They took a long break," the birds opened their wings and started to fly in the order they landed in. Wiping my eyes and looking at them in bewilderment, I muttered, "Why did they look as if they were flying with their tails a moment ago but now with their wings?" The front one vectored to the side.

Taking his place and leading the group, the bird opened and closed its yellow beak and answered my question, "We were in a hurry to get to this stop, so we made our tail a propeller, too."

While I was wondering if it was an audio illusion, I muttered, "They're listening."

"Of course I hear you," said the voice on the other side of the receiver, as my ears were ringing. For a while we both listened to the silence on the phone. In that moment of silence, I looked towards the birds on the screen. Again, there was another change of leadership. The bird in the middle of the ring was really beat. It seemed as if it would fall out of the sky with every flap of its wings. While the others were flapping their wings, they didn't take their eyes off him. There was a strange doubt in their eyes.

After a while, the doubt in their eyes began to haunt

me. "Last night," my brother's voice said, faltering as I clung to the receiver firmly in my ear.

"Last night?" I asked as my gaze fell on the back of the birds.

The voice of my brother coming from the opposite direction, "We brought him home from the hospital in the evening," fell silent again. The birds had crossed the middle of the valley, embellished with deep and lush trees. The flock leader changed again.

"What happened after you brought him from the hospital?" I asked in a trembling voice.

Emitting from the opposite side of the receiver, my brother's trembling voice replied, "A few hours after I brought him home, his pain got worse."

I looked towards the white wall on which we were leaning the cabinet we had placed the phone on. The flowers in the white-framed picture standing in the middle of the wall began to disappear one by one. He muttered, "Is there something strange about me too, or are the things I'm looking at strange?"

I turned back towards the TV. The end of the valley was in sight. But the bird in the middle no longer had any strength. The birds begin to narrow their circles even more as something inside me said, "The valley must end." As they narrowed their circle, the bird in the middle began to flap its wings with its final strength, as if it comprehended everything.

"What happened then?" I asked my brother, blowing

into the receiver.

Coming from the other side, my brother's voice was mixed with the buzzing of the phone for a while, then he said, trembling, "It's about midnight." He swallowed and fell silent.

I looked again at the painting on the wall with my teary eyes. The flowers I saw just now have completely disappeared. A sparkling eye resembling my mother's eye, and long black eyelashes resembling my mother's around the eye appeared in place of the flowers. There was no pupil, but in its place was a faint line.

Ignoring my insensitivity, my brother's voice on the other side of the receiver said, "Today, after the noon prayer," but he couldn't finish his sentence.

When I heard the word 'prayer,' my gaze began to twitch between the birds on the screen and the picture on the wall. When my gaze twitching stopped for a moment, the image of a clean-dressed hodja in a turban appeared before my eyes. The hodja walked slowly to the front of the congregation.

Clearing his throat, "uh, uh," a few times as if tuning his poignant voice, he urged those behind him to stand in lines. He cried out "Bismillah!" in a high-pitched voice and began to recite a surah verse. The surah ended by the time the echo of the hodja's voice had reached those in the back row. After the verse, he raised his arms and touched his thumbs to his earlobes while saying, "Allahu Akbar" (God is Great). He paused for a short while, then called out, "Allahu Akbar" again. As those lined up behind him repeated what he had said, sounding off like thunder resounding in the void.

Hearing the sound, the blue sky imploded like a deflated balloon. As the blue sky shrank, the birds that appeared on the screen narrowed the circle even more and joined their wings and took the middle bird on their wings.

When the hodja's voice said "Amen," those who stood in line praying walked towards the coffin made of white pine, the scent of which my mother loved so much. When the first to reach the coffin lifted it and walked forward, the hodja and those behind followed them with shortened steps. Those carrying my mother's coffin were in the front, the hodja and the congregation were walking behind them, as the black-clad men carrying Leo's coffin pushed it into the mouth of the burning furnace as I had just closed my eyes in my bed, the priest crossed himself and said, "Amen." While the birds on the screen were screaming with their own voices, the hodja told the congregation, "Let's give her a Hail Mary."

The congregation replied in unison, "Hail!" as a white-winged angel resembling my mother appeared next to the eye in the picture on the wall. Her hair was the color of my mother's, but light and messy. When in fact, my mother always combed her hair and hid it under a headscarf. The hodja put his hand on the soil that covered my mother and began to recite a Koranic verse for a long time.

After the verse, he said clearly, "Al-fatiha for her soul···"

When he finished reciting the Al-fatiha, he softly said again, "Amen."

The people around the grave gave a long, "Ameeen" in unison, extending the word. Then, overcoming their momentary astonishment, they all got up and walked hastily in the direction they had just come from.

While the hodja was alone at the tomb, the birds on the screen had reached the end of the valley. With the hiss of the one in front, those in the circle suddenly widened the formation. As they widened their circle, the tired old bird they'd borne on their wings began spiralling down into the depths of the abyss at the end of the valley. Momentarily confused as they dispersed this way and that, the birds began flying in the direction they came from, hastily flapping their wings, not unlike those in the congregation who had laid my mother in her grave, and double-timed in the direction where they came from.

As I looked after them, I said, "You know, they used to say that mountains don't meet mountains, people meet people···" and then I said, "So that's how they were fooling us···"

Refugees

I

I was washing my face in the sink when the phone rang. Grabbing a towel, I ran into the living room. When I picked up my cell phone on the table, I recognized that soft voice coming from the other end. As soft as ever, it was both trembling and anxious.

I think there was some crying mixed in it as well, "Son," she said. "My sooon," she said, stretching out the word.

"Mom," I replied as if I'd forgotten myself.

"Son," she said, regaining her wits. And after sighing, she said, "There's nothing here without you," sighing for a while. "Didn't you read the newspapers?" When in fact, the first thing she did in the morning was read the newspapers.

"No, Mom, this is another world, I can't do any of the things I did there. Besides, the newspapers published here are totally different…"

"What do you mean?"

"It'll take us three days to read what you read today."

"Isn't that Europe over there?"

" I don't know, Mom, I haven't seen the Europe mentioned there yet. Maybe I'll see it later, I guess."

From my mother's silence, I could tell she was confused.

"What was in the papers that made you cry, to confuse you like that?" I asked, in order to understand what had confused her by making her talk.

Softening her voice even more, "Do you see my tears, son?" she said.

It was her time to be confused and quiet. Mother said, "Since you're not amongst them⋯" then fell silent.

After mulling it over my mind, "What happened to Mom?" I persisted.

"Mom, what was in the papers?"

"I heard your voice, it doesn't matter what is written in the newspapers."

"But Mom, you're just consoling yourself, but you're worrying me."

As if extricating the words from her mouth one by one, "A tractor-trailer overturned around your place!"

"Trucks overturn here every day, Mom⋯"

"But it was like you in this truck⋯"

Involuntarily raising my voice, "Mom⋯ Like me what?"

"There are refugees like you."

"Well!"

"You're not amongst them, that's important to me, son."

"Mom, what happened to them?"

"Most of them are dead."

While I was holding my breath, Mom said, "You're important to me, son."

"But they had mothers too⋯"

"Every mother cries for her own son first."

This time I sighed. My mother did as well. She immediately changed the subject.

After saying something indiscernible for a while, she said louder, "I missed you so much, son. Hearing your voice is enough for me for now."

Hearing my voice from her trembling voice meant that she was looking to convince herself that I was alive. She didn't hide it either.

"Hear your voice. I called to convince myself you're alive," she said.

My mother had nothing else to talk about. My mother wasn't the only one; I'd also run out of stuff to talk about. When in fact, every time she rang, she'd ask what I was doing at that moment, and I'd tell her down to the smallest detail. These days, she no longer asks, nor do I want to tell her. My mother's intuition was very strong. From the words and phrases we iterated, she immediately understood the cold wind blowing between us. Beating a hasty retreat to leave me alone with me, as she does at times like these:, "I'll call you later," she said.

Since the day I set foot here, I started to look like the people here. My mother was always looking for me. Even though I wanted to call, I was always considering my budget. When in fact, my mother also received her monthly retirement payment and she was calling me with her surplus, I said, "Okay Mom," and hung up the phone.

After my mother's phone call, I went to our people's

ghetto in the north of the city, even though it wasn't my custom. Though I'd searched for news about the overturned TIR, even looking at the advertisement pages of many newspapers that I'd only glance at the first page, I couldn't find it in any of them. Perhaps there was something in the German newspapers, but I couldn't read them now. I couldn't find any news about the overturned TIR in the newspapers that day or the following day. On the third day, as soon as I had my breakfast, I went to that coffee shop where various newspapers were sold. It was the best way to read a variety of cheap tabloids. Anyways, it was impossible to find our newspapers in my neighborhood.

I was stunned when I entered the coffee shop. Despite being early, the place was packed. I walked over to an empty table in a secluded corner. I had just sat down when the waiter came. After I had my tea, I started checking out folks reading newspapers. If someone finished reading one and laid it on the table, I was going to snatch it up immediately. If only I could get into the swing of things, the rest was a piece of cake. After a while, someone was called to join a game. I immediately dashed over to grab the paper he had left. I straightened up the jumbled pages of the newspaper and started from the headline page. My mother was right to be alarmed. Almost all the first page was devoted to the news of the overturned rig. There were bloody bodies on the ground. Injured people, their bloody hands raised, as they begged for help, women with torn clothes lying face down, unknown whether they were dead or alive··· I shuddered. The license plate of the overturned semi caught my attention. It was the same one that brought us here months ago. I shivered and shuddered again. With that shudder, I peered intently at the pictures.

I was reading the captions under the pictures when I heard the sound of a large stone amber rosary coming from very near me. Rosary beads were clattering nonstop, as if there was nothing but that monotonous sound heard in the coffeehouse. I heard the sound and realized that someone was standing next to me. I think he was bizarrely chomping on gum. Contemplating whether or not to turn towards him, the man pointed at the pictures with his fingers holding the beads.

While showing, he stopped his masticating and said achingly, "They brought them all to our hospital."

Showing a man lying in blood, "But this one had too many injuries, they operated on him immediately. After a day of keeping him waiting downstairs, they took him into the operating ward. Now he's got neither arms nor legs. The nurse said he would've died had they not amputated on him.

"Do you work at the hospital?" I asked him.

"Yes I do," he said, sitting in the chair opposite me. After rotating his beads a couple of times, "I felt weird when I saw my homie like that. He was just like a log. He had no arms, no legs. Just imagine a baby groaning in bandages··· I don't think he's gonna live very long."

"Are you a doctor in the hospital or do you do another job?"

He grinned through his nose.

Who am I, not a doctor, that's for sure, my friend. I'm just a janitor. I've been working in the same hospital for 15 years now. I've been in Germany for exactly 27 years. I came here because of my late-father. Well, he wasn't dead at the time. We just say that once our mouth is used to it. But even to call them dead is committing a sin. Why would I say that? Because, the day he took leave during the second year he was here, he started to dislike my mother. Just two years before that, he was calling his wife "my field," "my cultivator," "my farm," "my plow." I was 13 or 14 years old. I wanted to take a sharp pitchfork from the courtyard and plunge it into his stomach. But he was pretty strong. That's what we did that year. The next year, when he went on leave, he began to humiliate my mother and I even more, constantly harassing her, "Are you a wife too? Those beautiful German wives, besides their beauty, put on all kinds of scents while entering the man's bosom. "You smell nothing but sweat," he exclaimed. Having reached the end of her patience, my mother, fired back one day.

She said, "If you brought me one of those good scents, I'd wear it too, man."

We couldn't comprehend what happened, but he

grabbed my mother's hair as soon as she got up, "So you want a scent, huh? They smell like bitch, bitch⋯"
My mother, who was furious, suddenly smacked my father in the face so hard that blood started to pour from my father's nose.

While looking at them, confused about whom to help, my mother said, "Either you choose the scents of bitches, or the scents of my sweat. Tell ya what, I won't even make you sniff that sweat you don't like from now on," she barked.

In the years after my father returned from that summer leave and came to Germany, he neither took leave nor did help us. To every letter we wrote, he'd reply, "I couldn't work this month, I won't be able to send the money you want. Forget about me, and take care of yourselves. I hope I'll work next month⋯"

We'd also sent a letter again asking for money in the hope that he worked the following month. He was writing and sending almost the same letter as he had a month ago. My mother and I were both helpless and confused. Because the number of my brothers and sisters my mother put in her belly every leave was quite high. We couldn't earn enough even if we both worked day and night. And besides, my mandatory military service was approaching. Fortunately, my mother was a talented woman. She persevered and increased her two cows to four and her five sheep to ten. She also boosted the amount of seed to plant in our fields.

I also went into the army in those years of abundance. When I came back from the military, everything had gone topsy-turvy. It was as if my mother had aged ten years. If you grabbed a patch of one of my siblings, you'd rip off forty patches. It's a shame it all happened in just two years. From my hunched-over shoulders, my mother sensed my discomfort.

" It hasn't rained a drop since the day you left. Neither prayers nor sacrifices got it to rain. Two drops haven't fallen in two years, son. Those animals that we multiplied and slaughtered contracted foot-and-mouth disease. The soil swallowed our seeds, and only grew an inch tall, then it all dried up. The disaster that strikes once in a hundred years has befallen us in just two years. No matter how much we wrote to your father, he didn't reply to a single letter of ours. I took pictures of the children and put them in the last letter, in case he might see the light, but the man's heart was hardened and his feelings were stone, so we received no word. Who knows, maybe he died there."

"The fact that he might be dead touched me. I don't know why it touched it, but it did. Still, I didn't cry. I cried since I was a child, but my crying was to no avail. So is begging. When a person cries or begs, he only consoles himself for a moment. Besides this, this is absolutely no good. I didn't cry, but just in case it might have helped my sobbing mom a little, I said,

"Well, if he doesn't come here, if he doesn't write to us, I'll go to him."

I borrowed some money, then hit the road. I was able to find my father only after going through Hell. He was living a good life with a German woman. I was ashamed to enter their house. I sat on the sofa with my feet under my butt because my feet stank. I was ashamed of my smell and my poverty, which was visible from my tattered socks, but my father didn't give a shit, proudly pointing me to his wife, calling me "my son."

My father couldn't think so sensibly, but when the German lady saw me sitting in destitution, she smiled at my father, saying, "Ismail, look, your son isn't comfortable. Tell him he's my son, because he's your son. Tell him to relax as if he were at home."

While my father translated the words of the woman I didn't understand, I felt as strange as when I saw that limbless man. I said that there was nothing dead about my father. The man showed no real appreciation for that nice German woman, either. If it were up to my father, he'd have stuck a few pfennigs in my pocket that first day and sent me home. But that German woman found me a janitor job. Thanks to that job, she got me my residence permit. So that's how I ended up staying. No matter where you are in the world, you'll always find some good folks, my friend. As it is, aren't we living in this world for the sake of *good people? After that first job, I worked in many jobs until I found this hospital job. This job is also a cleaning job, but it's not like that. There's clean dirt, too.*

He looked towards the waiter. I thought he was going to order some tea, but while he looked at the waiter, he flipped a few of his rosary beads and returned to his conversation, "My sonship ended the day I started work. That's also when I started being a father to my father. Do you have any idea what it means for a little man to grow up all of a sudden, who didn't even know the tiny environment he lived in until that day? But how would you know? Let me explain briefly. If you're a small person, you have the right to try everything once. Everything you can imagine. Even love. If you fall in love, you're obliged to marry. That's because you have the courage to do everything once. My fellow countryman, I'm sorry if I'm yakking my head off, but I've got so much to get off my chest. Something came over me when I saw that quarter of a man. I always looked at him when I went in and out of his room. He only had his eyes. I can't tell if they were alive or dead. Luckily, he's in a good hospital. Thank God, one of the doctors goes in and out of his room. Even important university faculty members visit his ward with their students to examine him. I don't know why, but those students gape at that limbless log the way kids stare at lions at the zoo. He *stood up after thumbing his amber rosary a few more times. He glanced at his watch as if showing off his expensive Rolex wristwatch.*

He smiled at me, saying, "My dear fellow countryman, it seems you won't be going to work today. I need to be getting to work. But before I take off, let me tell you what happened to my father, in case you're wondering. Do you know what happened? Just as they wrote for many before him as, "the first expat to die of AIDS," one day, our newspapers wrote that my father was "the first expat to die of AIDS."

Well, that's about all for now, I have to head off. Boy, it sure feels nice getting all that off my shoulders. Wow, you're a great guy, you listened to all that without saying anything, man. Well now it's time to go. Let me go and see what our log's doing. No one else but me is aware of him, the poor sap. How would I know if I didn't work at the hospital?

It sounded as if he was talking about a real log when he said that. I looked behind him as he walked away. I went to the coffeehouse early for four days in a row after that and waited around until late for him to show up. I thought I'd get some news if he came. What a putz I was, why didn't I get the address of the hospital, and the ward number the man was in? I was just sitting in front of him like a frozen blood popsicle while the guy laid it on the line. I spent four long days blaming myself like this, expecting him to show up at any moment. Of course, I drank tea morning, noon and night so I wouldn't be a shame to the coffeehouse. By day five, I'd given up hope he'd show up.

Just as I was getting up to go home, he straightened his hat and came inside. He was wearing a hat just like Attila İlhan's. After all, only his hat had changed from the peasantry he had brought with him years ago. Everyone at the cafe knew him, and vice-versa. But the grins of everyone who saw him got my attention. It seemed as if everyone was greeting just to poke fun of him. But the truth of the matter was, he was poking fun at everyone. Searching for a place to sit at other tables, he couldn't find one to his liking, so he headed over towards mine. I also gave him a fat grin. I also offered him some tea, not wondering if I'd have enough pfennigs in my wallet to cover it.

After asking how he was, I brought the topic of the "log," as he put it.

Taking a sip of his tea, he spun a full turn of his rosary beads for what seemed like an eternity to me.

"He's not good at all. He still lies there like a log. Yesterday I went into his ward singing a tune. I forget everything once I start working. Anything but thinking that the job is about making money. Making money here is the best and most important thing in the world for me. That's what my happiness is. In that happy moment, I forgot all about his pain and was humming a song I knew. There was a tall nurse next to him. It was as if his eyes lit up as he stared at the voluptuous blonde nurse's butt. I went over to him when the nurse exited the ward.

Shaking my head, I admonished him, "Hey grumpy, how about keeping your eyes to yourself, and not on the nurse's butt!" I got a little closer, so I could chide him and console him a bit, as well. I bent over him, thinking he couldn't hear what I said with his ears all bandaged up like that. I looked into his eyes as I bent down. Guess what I saw then?

II

This is the third country I've been to. Where will I go if I'm not accepted here? I've got no other place to go. It's been exactly six years today and I have yet to find a country for myself. Ever since I saw how the corpses of the Chinese suffocated in that truck, I no longer dare to go to another country. Then the human traffickers work with shackles. It's been two years since I lost the link in that chain. Even if I try to find it now, it would take me at least a year. What happens if I try? It's impossible for me to give them the money they want, because they increase their wages every year. The men don't even lift a finger for anyone until they get their money··· Whenever I set out from my country, I thought that the Bulgarians would take care of us because they're my comrades. But we couldn't even stay there for three days. Moreover, in those three days, the men robbed us and took us for everything with we had. Then the Romanians, followed by the Hungarians did the same. What a dreamer I was··· I wish I hadn't been there, then my job would've been easier here. Then the places would've remained as they were in my own thoughts, and it would be a consolation for me. It seemed that the more countries I passed through, the smaller my world got. When in fact, as I embarked on my journey, I was telling myself that I was opening up to the world and that my thoughts would be enriched. I was right to resist going abroad for years.

Even on those rainy days, I was still undecided, but Mother was saying every day, "Son, you stayed on the roof all these years, they took you off the roof, but now they stuck you in the house. They say we've forgiven you, but if someone else accuses you, they'll put you through the wringer again. Look, you can't move like you don't live in this world! Like sons of other people, I want you to do what you want. You've done a lot of schooling. You can make a living wherever you go in the world. You've always broken my heart until now. And you'll break it up some more I guess. But I'm afraid for you. I'm afraid they're going to fill your void with a madman we know. Even if he does nothing, he'll set our house on fire in the middle of the night. You know, there's not much difference between sleep and death. We'll both burn to ashes. I'll sell off a few sets of your father's heirlooms. That money will take you to the end of the earth. Don't worry about me, I still have the other kids. The year will pass if I stay a couple months in each of their homes. I'll get by on your father's salary. I lived very happily with your father. Your siblings built their own homes, and had they let you go, you would have built one as well. But it didn't happen. Then your choice was your destiny. Now's not the time to bitch about it, so go far away. It's enough for you to take a piece of my broken heart with you. I'll live thinking you'll return one day. But if they take you up onto the roof again, I'll have no such hope. So, get a grip already. What you call home is all pretty much the same⋯ Go far and put some time into doing what you want, and eventually, people will get your drift. Then you can come back home and start where you left off. Look, I didn't know much about these matters, nor about my own life, but your life taught me a lot. C'mon, take my advice, and do something other than just being cooped up reading books all the time."

Mother really wisened up in her old years. Having first said, "Don't drop your textbooks to read romance novels," Mother got used to the fact that books were my best friends years later, and I was surprised. After making sure a few times to see whether she really wanted me to go, I decided to go abroad. I searched for the organization again for a while, but instead of the organization, I fell into the clutches of smugglers. I struck a good bargain with them. After years of imprisonment, they didn't notice my departure, as I didn't make a scene leaving the house. Now here I am sharing this room with someone. As my mother said, they had locked me up in another room outside. But the place I got stuck in was a house. He had a room that belonged to me. Forget about a home of my own, I was now stuck in half a room. Anyways, my roommate and I are from totally different worlds. He can't understand me, and I can't talk with him. I go outside at every opportunity to rid myself of the solitude that has enveloped me, but to no avail, as it follows me regardless where I go. There's no one I can talk to whenever I duck into the coffeehouse, or the pub. I dropped by the pub again the other evening. Shadan had just started her new job. Our guys started to fall one by one. Those who knew me were greeting me first, and winking at the others from behind my back.

A man I'd never seen before entered the pub and approached the bar. He first peered into Shadan's eyes. She continued to wash the glasses without paying him any heed. The man suddenly banged his fist lightly on the bar. After which he shouted, "It's all your fault," as he glared at those who had just come over to sit around the same table. He banged again on the bar counter, this time more forcefully. On the middle finger of his right hand was a gold ring with a large gemstone. "It's all your fault, you sons of bitches," he said coarsely.

The others looked in askance at the man. Shadan shimmied on over to the table balancing a tray full of drinking glasses.

While the man's eyes wandered over Shadan's attributes, one of the people around the table said, "Give something to Hasan too, Shadan···

The man said, "You can't get that stone out with a drink like that."

The one drinking said, "Just get a couple of swigs in you, then we'll talk, Hasan. You must be parched···"

Hasan interrupted the speaker, "I'd rather drink my own piss than drink your pissant drink··· You weren't going to do this to me··· You wouldn't have done it before, but now you all act like a bunch of cunts.

After an interminable wait, he exclaimed, "You're just as full of crap as everyone else who hangs out here." When I got a call from friends I'd arranged to meet a week ago, I left that evening without seeing how this game ended. As if there wasn't anywhere else to go, I went back to that pub the very next evening. They were all there again. Recognizing an educated person when they saw one, they managed to demonstrate a modicum of respect. It didn't matter to them whether it was called respect or continuing a tradition, but being a pal was enough to perk their interest. Again, they competed with each other, blanketing the table in front of me with drinks in a matter of minutes. Someone must've noticed something missing, as he ordered some nuts. I wouldn't be able to drink it all because my head's not cool with an onslaught of beverages, but I didn't reject any of those who came because I knew the hospitality contest between them. I took turns with them saying "cheers" and raising my glass. They were thrilled. I already knew them very well. Making one happy made them all happy. Of course, wanting to fight with one meant fighting with all of them.

Hasan arrived late. He looked over to their table and laughed, then came and sat next to me as if we'd been friends of 40 years. This time, the others competed to buy Hasan a drink. I never knew who Hasan was. I've never seen him in any coffeehouses I'd been to. He got right into it, saying, "These kids love you so much, go ahead and do a job."

"I only see them here or in coffeehouses, I've got no friendships or anything happening with any of them⋯"

"But they know you well⋯"

"Could be, but I don't know them⋯"

"You know something? They were just like you when they first got here. They liked to sit alone and contemplate their navels. But their worlds changed after we introduced them to our kids."

"How so?"

"My goodness, you're one slick dude. You pretend not to let on, but you don't miss a thing, do you?"

"Hey, I don't know you all that well⋯"

"No worries. We can touch bases later on. I'm a patient person, I know very well how to wait and chill. I've met a lot of folks who say they can't and won't change. What are you going to do later if you don't change?"

"What do you mean?"

"Look, homie," he whacked my shoulder.

After taking a sip from his drink, he added, "You better find out before it's too late!"

"What's that?"

"What the system wants from you and that it won't acknowledge you if you don't assimilate. You need to do that. Like them, you'll resist until you learn where your money comes from. Once you learn that way, you'll start resembling those here. Do you know why they haven't give your residence permit yet?"

"No, I don't, why?"

"The reason is they're waiting for you to empty yourself. Once you reach the consistency they want, that's when they'll lay everything under your feet. At first, they always try to improve with less. If they're successful, they'll show that success to most people. Let me say that instead of being happy with the little they're giving, you've got to move towards their own abundance. It's like our ancestors once said, 'Strength comes from unity.' If you join us, you won't be wasting your time."

Taking a sip from the glass in front of him, we then both raised a toast to those sitting at the opposite table.

Turning to me, he said, "Look, I've got to get up early in the morning, come to our coffeehouse tomorrow and let's talk. Until then, I'll catch you later."

Then he got up.

To the barmaid Shadan, he said loudly, "I got my

friend's tab," and left.

He did most of the talking while he sat there, and I was only able to get in a few questions. I don't know why, but as soon as he left, I began wondering whom he kept referring to as "ours" in the middle of his banter.

While I was mulling this over, Dervish, whom I knew from the coffeehouse where I dropped by almost every day and played games once in a while, entered the pub. Spying me, he came over and took the seat Hasan had just vacated.

Looking at me, he asked, "How ya doing?"

Eyeing the glasses on the table, he added, "By the looks of all these glasses, I guess you're doing alright."

I peered into his face. "You're pretty much the only one I know here. If you know me even just a little, you'd know I'm not a big drinker. I'm not sure why, but the guys at the next table always compete against each other to buy me rounds every time I come here. I don't turn down what they send to my table so I don't get on their bad side."

Dervish gave me a beady look. Then he turned to those sitting at the next table. Without turning back at me, he said, "They're right, they see in you their old selves from years ago. They probably think you can accomplish what they couldn't···"

"I don't get your point."

"Never mind, we got it, but what happened?"

"Dervish, the owner of the Friends Coffeehouse, Hasan

was just here. He mentioned some mysterious stuff then left. I didn't get his drift, either. Now you're saying something, but believe me, I don't get you're drift either."

"I said, we get it, but so what? I think you should live your life as you wish."

"If they'd let me, I'd live exactly as you say, but they don't let it."

"You're an educated man, find a way to live as you want⋯ Ditch the refugee status."

"Why should I?"

"Because, our people disdain refugees⋯"

"I didn't become a refugee voluntarily."

"It doesn't matter⋯ just ditch it, and if you do, you'll see all the doors open⋯"

"Fine, so how do I go about doing that?"

"You gotta find a way to get free."

I didn't mean to say, "How can I break free?" Well, I've been declaring myself a political immigrant for years now, I meant to say, "How can I say 'I'm no longer a political refugee.'"

"For Pete's sake, you can't be that naïve!"

"No, I'm not, but why should I lie about it?"

"Our elders once said, 'You'll lie if necessary.' Are we any smarter than them? Who knows how long it took them to say that. Look, I'm not telling you to lie about anything. You're a cultured kind of guy, find one of ours and marry someone who's suitable for you. So, you can't find one that suits you, then find a Dutch girl. If you really don't want to get married, go the nuptial agreement route. That's good for three years max. Then it's clear sailing from then on. Your next life will be yours too. I can help too if you want. If you don't accept my help, just let Hasan know. He'll find you five in a week···"

Those who bought me a drink bought him one, too. Shadan beamed at his face as she placed his drink in front of him with svelte movements.

The purple lights illuminating the interior sparkled up her white teeth. Leaning a little towards Dervish, she asked discernibly, "Hey, Dervish, why haven't you taken us out for a fun time lately?"

Dervish glanced at me evasively, "I've been really busy lately. Winter's around the corner, then I'll have plenty of time."

They called Shadan over from other tables.

When she left, Dervish remarked, "Everything's good to go. Say she's got a great figure, call her flirty, call her fun, call her feminine, call her whatever you want. She spreads joy wherever she goes. Look, this can happen for you, too. I can talk with her if you want. She wouldn't want to become too attached, mind you, but she'll agree to a nuptial agreement. She wouldn't cause money problems like the Dutch, either."

III

It had been five or six years, and I'd missed my husband. When he told me to come, I packed up all my stuff and hit the road. My husband got me my residence permit not long after I arrived. They made it easy for him to get my residence. We applied to leave the camp as soon as possible and find a job after my residency was settled. We were in a hurry as the birth was approaching. We had also agreed to a one-room flat in Athens, but we couldn't find one. Confused about what to do while waiting for a suitable flat to be found in the camp, my pains started. My husband informed the camp doctor. The doctor and a nurse arrived together. Having poked fun at us every time we visited the doc, the nurse became a different person when she heard my screams.

After the first intervention, the doctor informed me, "Your birth's going to be a tough one, Zehra."

She had learned Turkish because she'd been working in this camp for years. In our previous visitations, we communicated with my little English, her little Turkish and the little Greek my husband was able to learn. But this time, he was speaking with his actions, not his voice. I sensed concern from the movements of his face and the way he spoke to the nurse. When my waters broke, my eyes couldn't see anything, but at other times I was always watching her. At one point, he said something to the nurse and left our tent and shack.

After a while, as she wiped the sweat off her forehead, he walked in, saying, "The hospitals were full, but I was still able to arrange an ambulance. It'll be here soon. You keep taking those deep breaths."

The words he said were unlike his usual speech; it was as if he was going to say something else. But I wasn't in a position to ponder the secret of his words. I was screaming all the time. Sweat was pouring off of me. But nothing was helping the birth. He injected my arm with a pain-killer. After that injection, I thought the condition causing me pain would decrease, but I was wrong, my pain shot up. My screams increased, but a grin appeared on the doctor's face.

At some point, he said, "I guess there'll be no need for a Cesarean."

The wave of my contractions grew more and more frequent. I felt my hips expand as my contractions increased. That's when I saw the doctor's big black eyes sparkle with joy.

"C'mon push, Zehra," he said in a crisp voice···

I was able to see my child exactly three days after that difficult birth. The doctor sent her to the hospital with the ambulance, as she didn't react the moment she was born. As I regained consciousness, I gave up hope when he said he had transferred the newborn infant to the hospital. He said this to console me, and after a while I thought to myself that he'd say, "She died in the hospital."

Seeing my eyes watering, he consoled me, as if reading my mind, "No, Zehra, it's not what you think. She could've stayed here, but she needed to be in a sterile environment for a few days. You know this place too···"

He came to comfort me every day until my daughter arrived. I took solace in his consolation. But I couldn't control my breasts. They were throbbing because my baby wasn't suckling yet. I tried to milk them every once in a while but still couldn't diminish the throbbing. I suffered plenty until that little mouth came and suckled.

Even after our daughter arrived, the doctor both visited us and wrote a letter to the home office, saying, "The camp's unsuitable for the infant's health and care," and wanted to help us get a home as soon as possible, but those in the home office didn't even respond.

My daughter was really frail. If the doctor hadn't helped, we might not have been able to keep her alive. As we looked at our child, something broke inside both of us. I told Asım I wanted to return home with the child. But he didn't agree.

Our insides melted as he and I looked after our child, but we were doing our best not to show it to each other. But I started to blame my husband all the time, like he was the cause of everything. One day, my daughter's incessant coughs overwhelmed me. I lost my self-control, as I shouted, "I don't want to stay in this camp, in this country anymore."

Asım was dumbfounded. We lived for a long time fearful of his arrest in our own country, but here we were both imprisoned, and we didn't have a home to care for our child in better conditions. I packed my suitcase without worrying about anything. I wasn't listening to whatever Asim was saying. After bundling up my daughter, I went over to the doctor just to say "goodbye."

When he saw me with my bag and daughter like that, he asked, "Is she sick?"

I said that he knew everything, that if the child stayed in this camp, she wouldn't be able to develop, maybe she'd die. He said I was right.

Looking worriedly at my face, he asked, "So how are you going to get out of the camp?"

I said that if they wanted, I would return the residence permit they gave me, anything to leave this camp. He asked about Asim. Just as I was saying that he didn't know what to do when Asım showed up. He spoke a little Greek with the doctor. Or rather, the doctor did all the talking.

Looking at us with sad eyes after the doctor's speech, Asım said, "The doctor says, 'try to avoid going back to Turkey, go somewhere west.'"

His sad eyes must have enveloped me because I agreed with what he said. He was happy when we told the doctor what we thought. He smuggled us out of the camp in his own car, telling the camp officials, "The kid's sick, I'm taking them to the hospital."

We hocked my two bracelets from our wedding day and came to the Netherlands via Italy. Since Greece was still not a member of the EU back then, the passports they issued were no good for us. This time, the three of us became refugees together.

It was the third or fourth week of our application, they interned Asım and sent him back to Greece. I don't know how they found out, but they had learned that he had residence there. They didn't touch my daughter or me. They sent him from the temporary camp to the permanent camp. The camps here were very good compared to back there. My daughter and I had a fairly large room of our own. They were helping in every way because they understood my daughter's inadequate development. Within a few months, her body was beginning to plump and her skin to turn pink. I was afraid of hormone food and drugs, but I also liked my daughter becoming more robust.

In the evenings, I'd stretch out on the bed and have her lie on my chest, singing lullabies until she fell asleep. There was a ditty I made up myself that I sang almost every evening:

> *My daughter was born in a camp,*
> *His father is faraway*
> *What comes from afar*
> *Don't let love remain in the trap.*
> *Especially a gift*
> *My daughter's name is Hediye*···

Sometimes I couldn't put her to sleep with ditties, so I used to tell tales. She'd smile at me as if she understood. I could tell from her behavior what she wanted. Sometimes, no matter what I did, I couldn't put her to sleep, so I'd talk to her like a friend. One day I realized something. The kid was already asleep, but I was still talking.

In the first days, I was very surprised to see that most of the people in the camp were talking to themselves. In fact, I laughed bitterly at them. But now I was one of them, talking to myself. When you can't find someone to talk to, you talk to yourself.

The next day, I told Leyla sister, who was interned at the camp like me, "Last night, after my daughter went to sleep, I suddenly found myself talking to myself."

She chortled, showing her pearly teeth, "That's what happens when you end up in the camps for so long."

Since then, I increased the length of my conversations with my daughter even more. But the naughty girl was either doing other things or sleeping butt up, as if she was tired of my banter. For days, for months, we cuddled up together in bed. I had made my daughter chubby, but this time I was starting to lose weight.

The letter of the Ministry of Justice came around the time I thought that I had caught a bug from somewhere. My Dutch was as much as I learned in the courses, but I understood from the scales of justice on the envelope that's where it came from. I put it on the table and gaped at it for a while. I didn't know what it held, but even its arrival made me happy.

Then that was the first step. The second step would be to get free of the camps. My biggest wish was to get my residence and get some employment.

It was a weekend. We went to the house of someone Leyla knew. The host picked us up at the camp in his car. He had brought his family to the Netherlands years ago. More precisely, as the man said, they'd abandoned their plow in the field with the oxen and come here. Even their children had grown up. The way they viewed us caught my attention in that it was if they were gaping at a zoo animal. Although they lived in the same room and very close to us, they looked as though they were far away from us. It was as if there was an invisible mountain between them and us.

At one point it seemed to me that I'd never reach them. Most of all, I was disturbed by their girl's gaze. It was like she was looking at some personal belongings while looking at us. At one point, she followed her mother into the kitchen for a while. So I went after them to ask for some hot water for my daughter's babyfood. They didn't see me come in as their backs were facing the door.

The girl asked her mother, "Who are they?"

Her mother, who was no more than a displaced villager, replied, "Who else, our freeloaders."

Hearing what she said, I also gave up feeding my child formula and returned to the living room. Leyla's husband immediately understood that my return was not a normal one. He gestured in askance what happened. I gestured back that nothing happened. Nevertheless, saying I forgot my baby's medication, I asked if he could take us back to the refugee camp.

We had a cup of tea then he drove us right back to the camp. On the way, the man asked me several times if I'd been "offended by anything," but I didn't dare repeat what his wife and daughter had said. After he left, I told Leyla what had happened. From that day on, I'd been eagerly waiting in anticipation for this letter.

IV

I was more excited than he was when I looked at his face bent like that. Watching his lips tremble, I couldn't wait to hear what he had to say. But I was a little disappointed when only breath came from his lips, and not a sound. Without losing hope, I searched for something like a sound, a word in his breath. Even if I read a prayer I knew that there'd be something I wanted to hear, it didn't help. It was only his breath that came out of his lips. I was confirming my inner disappointment when I saw his eyelids move.

He paused for a while after scowling at me. Slowly he turned the large, loud beads of his amber rosary. He reached over and picked up the teacup from the table while he continued to scowl at me. The glass disappeared in his large hand. He took a few sips of his cold tea. He first extended the glass to his saucer. He suddenly gave up without putting the glass on the plate and gulped down the remaining tea. The glass clanged as he put it on the saucer.

Placing his hand next to his string of beads, he said, "I

often forget to drink the tea, and it gets cold. I don't enjoy drinking cold tea."

As I wanted him to hurry up and tell me about the log, I said, "The tea's no big deal. We can always order another one…"

I hadn't finished my sentence when I thought of the money in my pocket. My gaze paled. I stopped calling over to the waiter and looked in his face. I don't think he understood why I was staring, but somehow his jaw slackened.

Thickening his voice, he said, "When I looked into his eyes, I saw that his eyelids were opening and closing regularly. I paid closer attention. The man was talking with his eyes. I knew about this way of communicating, but from where?

Smacking myself on the head, I said, "What a knucklehead, you know it, figure it out!"

As the man opened and shut his eyelids in one long, one short, two short and one long, I recalled my military service. I was in transportation. They must have thought that out for me because I'm burly, I'd have no problems carrying stuff, so they delivered a magnetic battery to me right after the course.

At first it wasn't easy communicating with him, as it required some skill. When I saw the log talking with his eyelids like that, I thought back to those days when I first used that battery. I tried to remember the corporals, sergeants, master-sergeants, those who bullied me, those who taught me, those who looked down upon me as if I were a slug, those who swelled me up like an elephant, and tried to visualize the signs that I had forgotten years ago.

On the other hand, this man was talking··· I left the room muttering, "this guy's talking."

I couldn't sleep that night. Every time I closed my eyes, I was muttering, "Two dashes, one dot; one dash and two dots. Two dots one dash. Dash dot, dot dash. Dash dash dash. Dot dot dot···."

Anyways, a miracle happened··· I began to remember the letters one by one. My wife woke me up at night while I was deciphering conversations in a subconscious exercise. Before my wife woke me, my unit commander was saying, tell me the incoming message immediately.

Just as I was telling a message at attention, my wife woke me up, jabbing my side with her elbow. She was smacking me plenty hard··· It hurt, but I didn't mind. I shut my eyes again and watched the dots and dashes pass before my eyes. As if they weren't sounds but rather one short one long, one long one long marks.

The next day, I flew to work. I entered his convalescent ward while I was driving the battery-powered cart that was carrying my cleaning supplies. He was alone in the room. I was overcome by an odd feeling seeing him so alone. As I did the day before, I bent down and looked into his eyes. He was looking at me too. As he did yesterday, he was opening and shutting his eyelids long and short, trying to emulate Morse code.

I asked, "How are you?"

You should've seen how those beaming eyes of his··· I suddenly got excited and I had the feeling he was going to shout, "You understand me!"

I ran back to turn on the lights then came back to him. I bent down again and brought my eyes closer to his. We started communicating with our eyes.

"You understand me," he said.

"Yes, I was a transporter in the army, I said."

"I was topographer, too," he said.

I didn't understand.

Then he said, "Didn't you ever see those who measure and cut the hills and put signs there while the soldiers conducted exercises?"

"I saw them," I replied.

"They're topographers."

I didn't understand much, but I didn't want to appear ignorant to him either. I had been in Germany almost 20 years, and he'd only been here two days, so there was no way he was going to lecture me.

"Who are you?" I asked···

"I'm nobody," he replied.

"So you don't have a name?"

"There is, but it's good for nothing now."

"Why do you say that?" I said, "Whatever it's done for you so far, it will do for you from now on."

"Can't you see the shape I'm in?" he said.

"I see, what about it?"

"Do you think it makes any sense to live like this?"

I said, "Why wouldn't it? Maybe not in Turkey, but you'll see here, they'll have you wear artificial limbs and make you useful again."

"It's a bit difficult, but I hope it'll be as you say. But I'm not very hopeful."

"Why not?"

"I can't endure the pain on my right side. It seems like it's not going to get any better."

"Don't worry, they'll give you medication and heal that side too. Shall I call the nurse now?"

"After gesturing "No" and giving a very sad look, he asked, "What's your name?"

"It's Gulmehmet," I said.

"You're like a rose," he said.

I said, "Thanks."

"I want something from you," he said.

"Tell me, for God's sake, tell me, I'll do it right away," I said.

"What I want from you is···" he said.

He was silent for a long time··· I realized that he was crying because his eyes slackened.

My eyes welled up with tears as I looked at him. Chagrined, I said, "Please don't cry."

"You understand me very well," he said.

"I've been watching you for days, I think I'm very impressed."

"Don't think about me anymore, whatever happened happened. Just promise me something."

"What's that?" I asked.

"I want you to promise you won't tell anyone that we're talking in Morse code and that I feel everything"···

I looked at the ground···

"You won't say anything to the doctors."

"Why's that?"

"They think that I don't feel anything, and my brain doesn't perceive anything."

"That's not true," I said···

"It doesn't matter if it's true."

"Why is that?"

"Because if they understand that I feel and perceive, they'll prolong my suffering."

"Can't you bear the pain until you're well?"

"No, it's really unbearable···"

"But if we tell them, they'll give you medication and relieve your pain."

"No, my pains are beyond death. I don't want to live like this."

"So you want to die?"

"Yes!"

"Why?"

"It'll be better for me to die than to live like this. If I live, I'll cause the pain that I suffer myself, as well as that of those around me. I don't want this. Look, I'm like a pruned stump, as you say."

I had said that because I assumed he couldn't hear me. For perhaps the first time I was ashamed of my humanity. Anxious to shake off my embarrassment, I asked him, "Did you hear what I was talking about?"

"Not always, I heard it sometimes. That's when I heard the doctors say that the wound on my right side was gangrened."

"How did you know what they were talking about? You don't know German," I said.

"I finished the German high school, and then I continued studying at the university," he said.

"So you studied here?" I asked.

He said, "No." Then his eyes slackened again, this time I realized he was laughing.

"Why are you laughing?" I asked.

"You're in Germany, but you don't know there's a German high school in Turkey···"

I said, "Who taught me to know? Look how I learned what they taught me in the army. If they'd taught me, I probably would've learned it, too."

He didn't say anything. Neither did I.

His smile disappeared, and his eyes froze in a moment of indecision, then they moved again.

"You still haven't promised me you won't say anything to anyone. Come on, promise me," he said.

I don't know what I thought at that moment, but I said impulsively, "Promise, I won't tell anyone anything."

His melancholic gaze wandered around the room several times. Looking at me, he asked with his eyelids, "Can you sing the song you sang when you first entered this room for me?"

"Which song was that? I forgot···"

He blinked his eyelids and said the name of the song. I looked in his face and said, "Well alright, I'll sing it for you."

My eyes welled up. I was dumbfounded. I'm always like that when I'm going to cry anyway. Sometimes I'd argue with my wife, and take stock of the situation later. Then I'd pull away and cry inwardly. It was always like that before I cried. Ever since my stepmother introduced us, I've always felt so awkward in my arguments with my wife. We have three kids, but my wife and I still seem to be very distant from each other.

He fell silent as if he'd forgotten all he wanted to talk about.

I couldn't stand it when he took a long time keeping quiet, so I asked, "What happened to the log?"

A few days after I had talked to him, I went to work and was told that I was not allowed to enter the nurses' station. It was then that I understood his condition had deteriorated. I really wanted to see him one last time, but the doctors and nurses were coming in and out of his ward. I'd been keeping my eyes on them for a long time, then dove inside when I got a chance. The pain was seeping through his eyes. With a final effort, he said, slowly moving his eyelids, "My suffering is ending."

Seeing me frozen like that, he said, "I guess I won't be able to listen to you anymore, but just don't forget my tune."

The shape of his face changed from the pain. His eyes looked like they were about to pop out. His body shook in epileptic ecstasy. When his expression relaxed a bit, he hastily closed his eyelids, saying, "That's all."

V

I don't know whether I did a good or bad thing by sharing my room with him. He probably doesn't have any money. He doesn't say anything, but it's obvious he is destitute. It is 'round midnight. As soon as he arrives, he undresses in the dark and gets into bed. If he comes early, I'll ask if he wants me to take him to our garden. I noticed that he couldn't catch up to us, I'll tell my friends, and we'll gather up a box of tomatoes for him. There is more than enough work in our garden, as long as he asks for it. The work is a bit tough for him. I don't know whether he can bear it, but I'll demonstrate my humanity and extend my hand, and let him be the one to refuse. He's been here several days now, but we've only gotten in a few sentences so far. Years ago, I promised myself I wouldn't help anyone, but for some reason I want to help since the day he arrived.

When he came in late those first days, I was saying, "Oh, he's got nothing going on for himself, he can come around whenever."

I wasn't even looking at his vacant bed. But now, seeing his bed empty, I'm worried something's happened to him. From what I heard, Hasan's started to wander around his environs. Sometimes he'd send Derviş to check up on him in order not to arouse suspicions. How would the poor slob know they're the same person, and that they came to him for the same job? Back in our day, they were providing enough social assistance to refugees, but when the Berlin Wall came down, the situation here also changed. It seems to me that after paying rent for the room, he's only got enough money for tea and cigarettes. His only pastimes are smoking ciggies and drinking tea. I can't make sense of where all that water fits in that thin body of his. But I'm assuming that's how he suppresses his hunger. I used to not do it, but lately I've always been cooking for two. In the first days, he gave me an odd look when he saw the leftover food on the table. Then he got used to it. These days, I leave the breakfast items on the table. He eats as much as he can, and sticks what he doesn't eat back in the fridge.

The building's entry door opened. I can't hear his footsteps yet; I hear them when he starts climbing the stairs. None of the tourists stay out this late. I don't think it was anyone else but him who entered the building. He started climbing the steps. Yes, it's his footsteps. When he arrives, I'll pretend I've just woken up and say "good night" first, and then I'll have a talk with him. So what, we're just two people in one room. What are we going to do if we don't talk to each other? I also want to go out on the weekend, so maybe we can go together somewhere next weekend. I've been here for nine years, but apart from my previous acquaintances, I haven't met any new people, so thanks to him, maybe I'll meet someone new. I was a shepherd back in my village. I wandered with my sheep over all the mountains and hills in the region for ten months out of the year. Every now and then a lady would come around and I'd get to see some folks. Here, I'm surrounded by plenty of folks, but I still long for people. I'm sharing my room with someone, but we've only been able to speak a few sentences with each other for the past several days. Sometimes it feels like I was closer to people when I was on back on those mountains. No, this can't go on like this. Once he enters the room, I'm going to pretend that I've just woken up and talk to him for sure.

He doesn't sleep until I get back, especially on weekends. I know he waits for me. He wants to talk, but he can't say anything. I'm like him. I want to talk too, but I can't. We'll talk a lot once we start, but we can't start. It's like invisible mountains are between the two beds. We're two people in the same room, breathing the same air, but at the same time, we're two people buried in the same silence. It shouldn't be that hard to talk to someone. I'm guessing we're both just waiting for the other to break the ice. As such, there's this wordless silence between us. Who knows what he's thinking about me, what judgments he's making···

If he's awake, I'm going to talk to him tonight. If he's sleeping, I won't wake him up, but if he's pretending to be asleep, I'll first confront him by thanking him for the food he left on the table.

Once I elicit an appropriate response, I'll ask, "So, what was your name again?" Actually, the hostel proprietor told me but I forgot.

Maybe he's not going to want to talk. Nor is he going to be forthcoming with his name. Why would he be forthcoming with his name, he doesn't know me. It'll be better if I told him my name first. It's best if I ask him who Derviş and Hasan are.

For some reason, the people here don't seem to know each other, but they know all about each other. No, my dear, this one's not like the others. He doesn't seem as clever as the others. If I'd known his name, I'd ask a couple of acquaintances of mine about him. Boy, I'm making a big thing about it, I'll just go and talk with him. I'll enter the room, turn on the light even if he's asleep, wake him up, ask him things I want to ask, and answer his questions. I think it's a mistake we haven't done this yet. Let's not continue this mistake.

Now I'm sure he heard me open the entrance door and go upstairs. He'll watch out of the corner of his eye as I open the door of the room, slip slowly into the room, and undress with the help of the living room light and get into bed. However, I'm not going to do as he thinks tonight. I'm going to turn on the light the moment I enter the room. And when the light goes on, I'm going to look into his eyes. If he pretends to be asleep, I'll wake him right up. But, if he's really asleep, I won't wake him up, but in the morning I'll ask questions when he's having breakfast. I've got to talk to him, there's no reason why we're standing about like two blobs. It is absurd to seek a reason. Does there have to be a reason you can't talk to the person you share a room with? I think there's only one reason, and that's because I don't look like him. I studied all these years so as not to sound like him. No, no matter what happens tonight, I'll talk and get to know him. We're just watching each other, as if we're not two people speaking the same language. We're aware of each other, but we can't speak. But this silence will end tonight and we'll talk to each other. Who knows how many questions he's prepared to ask like me?

Both of them couldn't sleep with the discomfort of being unable to talk to each other while looking at each other's bed in the dark. The young man who had entered inside had forgotten the promises he made to himself outside, and while pointing his finger at the light switch, he withdrew his finger, saying, "If he's sleeping, I won't wake him up, I'll go and talk to him while I'm having breakfast in the morning," ignoring the looks he knew were watching him in the dark as he undressed and went to bed. But both had been tossing and turning in their beds for hours. Both covered in sweat, they simultaneously turned on their bedside light switches.

Kurban half-smiled as they looked at each other, surprised they had done the same thing at the same time. Without saying a word, he got up and went to the livingroom. He opened the livingroom window, looked out and lit up a cigarette. After taking a deep breath of fresh air coming from outside, he returned to the room.

Seeing that his roommate was still awake, he gathered all his courage to say, "I guess you didn't sleep well."

After a little silence, "We've been sharing the same room for several days, but we couldn't find the right time to get acquainted. My name is Kurban. What's yours?"

Slightly younger than him, his skinny roommate replied, "You're right, I arrive late, you leave early, and we never met. My name is Gürcan, I'm a refugee here."

"I know what it means to wait. They gave me my residence permit after making me wait exactly six years. It's been nine years this year. I'm longing for my daughter Çelime. I couldn't go back while I didn't have my residence, but now I can't return to the homeland with that refugee passport they gave me. So, as you can see, the longing continues. If I'd known it would take this long, I wouldn't have become a refugee. At that time, they said the easiest way to get your residence was to become a refugee, so I applied. When my friends who came with me as tourists found a job, they got their residency before me, but I waited for exactly six years. I don't understand anything about politics. I was a shepherd in the mountains before I came here. I threw my felt vest off my back and hit the road. I already had nothing but my felt vest. That's what I thought at the time, of course··· When in fact, I had so many things. For instance, I have my blue sky, my stars, my pipe, my sheep that listened to my pipe and went in whichever direction I drove them, my fragrant flowers here and there, the trees in which I sat as I wished, the springs where I drank my water, my wife who visited me once in a while and the air that I breathed for free, but I had these but I wasn't aware of any of them."

"Do you pay for the air here, too?"

"Yep. The guys have set up such a system that you even pay for the air you breathe. You might not be aware of it now but when you start going to work before the stars go out and you get your salary, then you'll see them all on your payroll stub. Can't we use our feet? Can't we just go outside to have fun? Do you think we can't see the bars? We see them but we ignore what we see to come back here and take refuge in our tiny room. Because if we don't, our hopes of reuniting with our children who think we're fathers because we send them money will be over."

"With that thought, I want to ask you something. Do you want to work?"

"Well, I never thought about it."

"Of course you're afraid of getting caught. They caught me three times in the garden with my refugee card, but they didn't send me back because there weren't many people working there. You're an educated man, and since you will not work in the fields like us, you'll have a difficult time getting your residence."

"I don't get it."

"As a shepherd like me gets it, you'll get it over time. Once again, I forgot, can you tell me your name again?"

"Gürcan…"

"Gurcan, bro, well, believe me, I didn't cast a single vote until I came here, but this place turned me a politician. Until they give you the residence they're going to give, they'll empty your heart to the extent you cease to be yourself and become someone else. More precisely, during that waiting period, they put such a fear into you that you can't get rid of those fears after obtaining your residence."

"I don't know your fears, but I have others. Maybe you didn't say it, but those who were refugees here before us told all the lies. That's why they think the truths I tell are lies. This is the third country I've been to. If they don't give me residence here, I've got nowhere else to go."

"Why, is the world over?"

"The world isn't over, but I'm done…"

"That's what most of those who came before you said. Most of them didn't get residence either, but their lives are much, much better than ours."

"I don't get who you're talking about."

"For instance, the ones who buy you drinks at the pub you go to every night."

"I'm not talking about living like them and I don't see any perversion in their lives. I think they deserve to have some fun, too."

"Let's forget about their lives, but you should know there are two ways to live here, either you become a cowardly rat like me, or you'll never get to ride a Mercedes like them."

"How's that going to happen?"

"You can start by hanging out with Hasan or Dervish. What's here that's greater than Hasan and Dervish…"

"What do they do?"

"What do you think they do?"

"I've only seen them a few times in the coffeehouse. And a few times at the pub I go to. That's why I can't say I know them much. We never talked about what they do."

"Look, let me speak frankly, none of them are bad guys. They're the best ones here, but if you get too close, they'll get you into narcotics. You can't understand how they get you involved. If you ask me how I know this, this place is the size of your palm. It's all word of mouth here."

"Can I call you Mr. Kurban?"

"Of course, but you can drop the "Mr." bit if you want."

"Mr. Kurban, I don't know why you didn't talk about this before, but I'm surprised you know so much. How do you manage to live in the center of the world while pretending to be outside of it?"

"If you call it that, so be it. Did you know, I only attended elementary-school. Then, as you know, I was a shepherd. But whether a person works as a shepherd or does another job, he always carries whatever is inside him. In the first years of my shepherd life, I always played other people's tunes on my flute. One night, after I herded the flock into a pen, I laid on my back, looking at the stars. A dog near me barked. I looked up and saw nothing. As I lay on my back and looked at the stars again, a star rose over me from among thousands of stars. I was suddenly caught in a light. I cried out, afraid of the light, and I jumped to my feet. I looked over at the pen and the sheep inside. Everything was in its place and the light was gone, too. While I was standing there so scared, I realized that my mind was opening like the blank leaves of a notebook and these lines were written on those leaves:

Will you play with me;
But don't be easy.
Because the flowers bloom inside out
I will give you the mountains.
On plains without stones
We'll stone the devil,
Tie up the mouths of the wolf packs,
We'll water our lambs.
Going to the land of the dead
We'll seek immortality.
The moon won't steal the light from the sun,
Phosphorescence won't hug the waves,
We'll be alone as we start the game,
Because love requires solitude.

These verses, I am sure, came to those blank pages of my mind with the star falling on my chest. A few of the words might've changed, but since that day I keep it in my heart and I blow it on my flute because this is my tune. Of course, you've also got a tune. Go on now, blow your own tune on your flute."

VI

After I put that letter, the contents of which I didn't know but was very happy to receive, on my desk and watched it for two days without touching it, I telephoned my translator Gülsenem. She was a lady who was like an open book and shared her joys with us. When I said there was a scales of justice emblem on the envelope, she jumped in her car and drove over. She joyfully entered our room in the camp and picked the letter off the table and sat on the chair facing me. She looked at the letterhead address for what seemed to be forever. She turned it silently in her hand for a while without looking at me. For a moment it seemed as if she had no intention of reading.

But when she slowly started to tear a corner of the envelope, I said to myself, "I was wrong, she'll open and read it."

She tore the envelope in half when she gave up on her work. Holding the torn envelope in her hand, she first looked at my daughter, then at me.

Wondering what to do, I hurriedly said, "Would you like some tea?"

"I'll have some, thanks."

In order to overcome the doubt in me, I rushed into the kitchen we shared with other refugees. I filled the teapot with water and placed it on the stove, then lit a cigarette. I've also gotten used to smoking lately. When in fact, back in my hometown, I'd have a fit whenever my husband came home, stinking the place out like an ashtray. But here I clung to the cigarette like a savior. I stayed in the kitchen until my cigarette was finished.

Meanwhile, the water on the stove boiled. I poured the water into a small teapot and tossed two bags of tea into it. With the teapot in my hand, I sprinted back to my room.

She left the envelope in her hand on the table and was playing with Hediye on our bed. She was spoiling the kid like there was no tomorrow. After letting the tea brew, I sat on the chair and watched them struggle for a while, then I poured the tea into glasses.

I said, "Gülsenem, I've filled your tea."

She must have understood what I meant, because she left Hediye, whom she had tired out, on the bed and came over. Taking a seat on the chair opposite me, she took two sips of her tea. She looked at Hediye, then at me.

After a few breaths, she said, "She tired me out···"

"She's used to playing. Women who left their children in their country play with them until the evening. You see, her job is to play until the evening.

"Oh, if Hediye been mine, I would've played with her until the evening."

"You're still young, take your time. If you get married, you'll have one like her too."

"I'll never have a kid," she said. Her eyes welled up.

"You told me you were single."

"I was married once and divorced."

I didn't like it at all, and I didn't want to ask anyone this question, but at that moment, it was as if my lips were loosened, and I blurted out, "Why?···"

She looked at Hediye. Her head hung forward, then down, without looking at my face···

"I was very young when I got married. I didn't know anything."

"Weren't you here? Is it possible to get married here as a child?"

"Zehra, when you look out of that tiny room, you view the world as big, but believe me the world's not as big as you think. Now look at this envelope. Maybe you think a lot's going to change for you with that letter in the envelope, But I don't think so. That envelope's going to give you some temporary happiness, that's all. That happiness is going to last until another unhappiness begins, then another happiness again. After that, a new unhappiness and it will go on.

I was 11 years old when I came here. My father was working alone at home, and he viewed us as something that hindered him, restricted his life, and was not so important to see. Perhaps the only good thing he did for me was to take my hand and walk me to school. I enthusiastically showed my primary school diploma to the principal. Without looking at my diploma, he asked my father my date of birth. I was very sad the diploma I received in my country was looked upon as something worthless. My father couldn't talk much to the lady principal··· They called a girl from the upper classes. She spoke for my father. Rather than eighth grade, they started me from seventh grade. I didn't know why, but I was very ambitious. From that day on, studying meant everything to me. As it was, we couldn't sit in the living room and watch TV whenever my father was home. He'd find an excuse to get furious with one of us, and he'd send us all to our bedrooms with that fury. We were three sisters and we'd share the same room. The house we lived had three rooms. Sometimes whenever my mom suggested we rent a larger house, my dad snapped at her, retorting, 'My income is only enough for here. You want me to work day and night? Even if everyone says it, don't you say that,' he said, turning down my mother's words.

"Years later, I understood the meaning of why he said, 'Don't tell my mother, you don't have the right to say anything.' My mother had given birth to seven children, six girls, one boy. None were living but us three. My father was angry with my mother for the death of his one son, and not the death of his four children. Therefore, the poor woman had no right to say anything. Still, we tried not to piss off our father because he brought home groceries and didn't leave us naked, we quietly retired to our room whenever he got angry.

"Dad's anger grew as we grew older. Customs we didn't see and didn't know of in our village began to enter our house. Seeing me flourish when I was in the eighth grade, dad said, 'You'll be covering up.' My mother was against that. You should've seen my father's anger that day. For the first time, he beat my mother, saying, 'I'm not going to let people call me disreputable.' I still didn't know what his honor concept was. After that day, I locked myself in my room and devoted every minute of my time to studying. I was the first in our neighborhood to graduate from the gymnasium school. Until then, no one, not even those born and raised here, had finished it. But I graduated. The only one thrilled was my mother. When we told my father that I was going to college, I thought he'd be happy. But instead, he looked at me with that castigating look, 'I pretended not to notice your studying until today. That's enough. You won't be studying from now on. You'll stay at home and wait for your fate,' he said.

"So, as if it wasn't enough that he destroyed my world, when I wanted to work, he took a club in his hand and confronted me, 'You see, I don't let my wife or my daughters go to work… We have so many relatives and acquaintances here, I won't put up with anyone looking upon me like I'm dishonorable,' he said.

"I couldn't understand what my father's honor was all about. I couldn't stop myself from outbursts of beating myself and crying in my tiny room.

"Looking for a way out of my misery back then, my mother implored, 'Sweetheart, no matter what we do, we won't be able to knock any sense into him. That's something you're going to have to cope with. There might be a solution if you pick the son of one of the prospect seekers who'll be calling on our house.' I decided to get married the day she said, 'If the young man you're going to marry is tolerant, he'll let you go to school, and you'll save yourself that way.' I was just 18 when I got married.

"We agreed that I could study with the young man I

married, but later on, he changed his mind, saying, 'Look, you don't need to study, my income is enough for both of us. You can stay at home, just give birth to beautiful grandchildren for my parents.' I ate humble pie in order to get them to allow my enrollment in university, saying, 'Fine, I'll give birth to grandchildren for them, but I'm also going to study until I have grandchildren.' They didn't accept this. I was unable to study or give birth. They traipsed me around to all sorts of doctors and hodjas, but I couldn't give birth to any grandkids for them. It was when the doctors said, 'You can't give birth,' that they started getting on my case. It was right around then when they chastised me, saying, 'What should we do with a bride who can't give birth?'

" Since I never wanted to return to my father's house, I begged them so much to let me stay with them, I even let their son marry someone else, but they refused. After the divorce, I solved my dilemma by moving to a city where my father couldn't find me. There, I found a decent job and I studied at the same time. I basically recreated myself. Now I'm here. I try to help everyone as much as possible, but I still feel the pain of the first day I started that school··· However, I tried so hard to render that pain smaller and get rid of it once and for all. I'm 32 years old now. Despite all my studying, I couldn't save my siblings from getting married at a young age··· They say my father is very sick, but I don't go see him··· I'd like to go but I can't. Every time I try to go, my feet go in one direction, and my heart goes in the opposite direction."

For a while, she drank tea without speaking. Until that day, I believed I was carrying the weight of the world, but after what Gülsenem told me, I learned there were others in the world living with their problems. Until now, I missed the outside without knowing what was waiting for me out there. But now I was starting to feel that desire was fading slowly into oblivion. Still, after so much suffering, I looked at the letter fondly, thinking it would let me catch my breath. Seeing at the way I looked wistfully at the letter, Gülsenem reached out and picked it off the table.

While trying to extricate the letter from the envelope, she complained, "I can't understand why they make the wide world so tough for us. We both graduated from university, and then I started working. Just as my husband was about to start working, he had to go abroad. So you see, like you, we couldn't seem to get our life started. The hope I attach to this letter is that it gives us the chance to make that start."

"I hope so."

As she refilled her tea glass and took a sip, she glanced at the open letter on the table, as if recalling something. After reading a few lines, she looked at Hediye, who was camped out on the bed amongst her toys. "If it's not for us, there might at least be some happiness for her," she remarked.

She placed the tea glass on the table and snatched up the letter. I tried to figure out her gaze, but I couldn't make any sense out of it. She read the letter to the end. She looked at Hediye again. Suddenly, she got to her feet and went over to the girl. She puckered up her lips and gently kissed her on the cheek. Then she tiptoed over to me so as not to wake the child and hugged my neck.

Moistly, she said, "Congratulations," For a while, our voices and tears of happiness mixed together. Turning around, she picked up the letter, saying, "C'mon, let's go see the camp guard while Hediye's asleep. Also, if there's a chance to move into a flat in the city where I live, let's sign there right away and wait for our turn."

I could only mutter under my breath, "What, Do we have take turns here too?"

Aristotle

I invited them to dinner, too. We'll be a party of three for dinner. I shouldn't arouse their suspicions.

If I act as usual, they probably won't get suspicious. But I have to do something to get them up early. It's best to say I'm tired when they come. Once I send them away, I'll start my work calmly··· I mustn't prolong it any longer. My intuition doesn't easily miss. I know I'll be unable to do it if I'm a little late. Whatever happens, it's got to end tonight. All this time I waited for the most opportune moment. Now I think that time has come. This would be a small consolation in return for what I've suffered.

I've never felt more ready than tonight. This evening's color and inspiration are unique.

I understood everything when I woke up in the morning. When I got out of my bed and looked out the window, the sun was pale but I didn't feel tired. As if that wasn't enough, I also got a letter in the afternoon. As soon as I took the letter in my hands, I realized that strange feeling which filled me. Even my breathing was trying to tell me something, the clouds busy shading the sun were waving from afar, whispering to me that my letter had arrived on a wing and a prayer, that they would come to my window to watch this night. There's no point in waiting too long or digging into the past. Everything is already side-by-side, it just seems like a piece is missing. Once that's completed tonight, the puzzle spanning a whole lifetime will be solved. From now on, nobody will be able to tell me to "sit under that light" anymore. Well, after all these years of waiting, I'll have done the best job I've ever done. But in order for me to be able to do that, I don't have to make anyone sense anything tonight. After all these years of keeping silent, my voice must be loud.

Now I have to get up. I must start preparing without wasting time. Everything should be ready by the time they arrive. They mustn't understand anything, they shouldn't perceive anything, nor should I do anything to create suspicion. Moreover, I shouldn't leave anything to chance. If they suspect anything, they'll either stick around until morning as if nailed to their seats or else get carried away like they used to. They'll start all over again before dawn. So, the earlier they go, the easier it'll be for me. I must send them off early so I can free myself of this darkness and accomplish this job without any rot. If they don't leave early, I won't be able to put the pieces together in time. If I can't do this in time, all the pieces will be scattered all over the place. Then I won't be me, I'll be divided into other selves and live in cities with submerged bridges. Even if my bones rot, they won't be of any use. From which grave did that ugly snake slither into my grave? Look how that jester grins? It looks like it's not going to approach at all, but it sneaks up on you as it sticks out its tongue and smacks its lips. How long can I hide fearfully from them in the bosoms of the king's daughters? Besides, the king's daughters can't protect me forever. And what's more, how long could I avoid the questioning gaze of everyone around me? When would the pity in those eyes go away? I'm not even sure whether it's they pity themselves or me. Anyways, from now on, nobody's going to pity me, nor will they add to the crimes on my shoulders. Tonight it'll all be over. It's all about me being able to bring those pieces together. I need solitude in order to bring them together. If I'm able to find the silence and put those pieces together, I'll stand up and blow in the face of even those at the top. Then when they boundlessly open their bloody eyes and gape at me, I won't look at any of them the way they do.

What if I call to tell them not to come tonight, if I say I'm ready to talk to you until the morning another time? No, it can't be later on. They'll also suspect something if I say, "don't come." The best thing to do is to let sleeping dogs lie. It's better they come. Maybe I'll catch something new looking at their faces. I've got to have everything planned out before they arrive. If I start without a plan, I'm afraid everything will go haywire. I'll have to go back the way I came. I have to prepare the food first and then the table···. Plates, cutlery··· Some white cloth napkins next to them. Next to it is a bottle of red wine. The wine's a great idea. Why didn't I think of that before? Red wine in a white bottle in the middle of the table. Two slices of toast with the wine. The red sunlight filtering through the wine reflects on the slice of bread like a bloodstain. Not like a fresh bloodstain though, as its color is darker than the color of wine. It stays in one spot as if it had dripped from the tip of a knife. Sometimes the light plays tricks, the blood standing in the same spot as if dripping from the tip of the knife disrupted by the play of the light. Its dark color is opening up and thickening. As we try to keep it between those two slices of bread, it turns into a raging river flowing towards us. As it flows rapidly, it continues to thicken and turns into an inexorable rushing river. As soon as it comes to me swimming in the raging waters of the river, its soft white hands hug my throat. While I'm struggling desperately, the others look at me and burst out laughing. When their laughter subsides, the two say in unison, "We knew it was going to hug your throat."

The river of blood drags us along for a while, then changes color to a dark tomb green as it flows backwards into its bottle on the table. I get up and put a single glass and a napkin next to the bottle. Next to them is the knife dripping with blood.

I have to get up and start work, but a football match has started on TV. The guys on our team are running well too. They'll win if they can run like that the entire game. Number 8, in particular, is playing really well. Just like a dream of the dead. No, my dear, a dream is both the property of a person who's asleep and something that flies away when he wakes up. It's best to compare his game to a lively, moving folk tune. But it'd be better if Number 9 wasn't playing. He looks like he's going to die if he runs. He keeps pushing himself, but his steps don't move forward. At least, there's Number 8. We can say that he's the star of the game. Look, he's all over the field. They've been trying to knock him down since the beginning of the game, but they still haven't done so. Look, he's passed everyone again. He's facing the goalkeeper. Wow, he's passed the goalkeeper. He's running, he's running. The goalkeeper is sprinting after him. The commentator is screaming at the top of his lungs. The running player is on top of the world. The opposing team's goalie's tongue is sticking out. Number 8 stops the ball and stretches. His leg is on the verge of discharging like a spring. But before he kicks the ball, he turns to look at the opposing team's goalkeeper, just to poke fun at him. "If he kicks with this stretch, he'll pierce the nets," screams the commentator, tearing his throat once more. Number 8 stretches a little more but gets excited. It's really unfortunate he's so excited. He's not sure what to do, just as he's about to kick the ball, the rival goalie leaps on top of it. Of course, this is what happens if you make fun of him. The commentator throat is torn, I guess he's lost his voice.

The bottle of red wine will sit on the table with its white tablecloth. Next to it is a white napkin. The bloody pointed knife is on the napkin. Maybe it's not blood dripping from the tip. That's because it also resembles dark red strawberry jam. No, jam doesn't go with wine. Where there's wine, there's blood. Either blood or wine!

The dining time stretches out, I distract them, and there's no time for chatting. Even when there's little time for chit-chat, we don't get carried away and forget the time. Meanwhile, I'll say I'm tired and send them off. I get into my pajamas when they're gone. Then I'll go and wash my feet too. Why would I just wash my feet when I can take a nice bath? Or could I still be afraid to go into the bathroom? At that time, I said I'd get into the bathroom in my pajamas and wash my feet then get out. Then I changed my mind. I filled the tub with water. I took off the pajamas I had just put on, and got into the warm water. The warm water loosened my muscles as well as the nerves embedded in my muscles. I lingered forever in the water. I took the towel in my hand to turn off the faucet and dry off when I heard that sound. I turned around and looked where the sound came from, no one was there. I had just wrapped the towel around my body when he reached out to grab the towel and pull it towards him. Startled, I looked back, but I didn't see him. I laughed out loud in utter fear. While I was laughing, I saw the image of the two of us in the bathtub water. I was scared shitless when I saw him looking at me. I started trembling. He started laughing when he saw me trembling. His head got bigger and bigger, his eyes bulged out, his teeth got bigger in the water. He got taller. His huge hands were about to catch my throat when the water rippled. Screams joined the sound of water as we struggled. Before the noises turned into growls, I don't quite recall whether it was he or I that went to the kitchen! We had a knife in our hands. I don't recall if it was in my hands or his. Suddenly, our struggle stopped as the color of the water changed. A shapeless face appeared in the rippling water. It was unclear whether the shapeless face was his or mine.

There was time for a cup of coffee. More precisely, it was a bit of time to take a sip from a cup of coffee. He owned that tiny piece of time. Like I am now, I was sitting, drinking my coffee. He slunk slowly inside, then came over and sat right in front of me. He kept saying "Aristotle Aristotle." He went silent once in a while, then chuckled incoherently. His chuckling was terribly disturbing. Once he reined in his laughter, he cleared his nose as if I hadn't noticed, exclaiming, "Aristotle, Aristotle!" as he stroked his furry black dog again. As soon as he said that, he burst out laughing louder than before. He rolled his bloody eyes and scanned me from top to bottom and vice-versa, shaking his head disapprovingly and contemptuously in the process. When he did that, I told him to his face that I didn't like him.

Hearing my voice, the whites of his eyes and his pupils mingled. "Did you hear that, Aristotle?" he said as he shoved the dog he'd been petting.

My eyes widened as he stood up and walked over towards me. "Everyone is precious with their own name," I said, looking at him. He pretended not to hear me.

He looked at his dog and beckoned to him, saying, "Hey, Aristotle, did you get that?" as if he was asking a person. I stood up and walked with my coffee cup in hand and stopped right in front of him. This time he looked at me like he was going to eat me in one fell swoop.

He grinned at "Aristotle" wagging his tail beside him. "Why don't you call the dog by its name, what's with Aristotle," I asked.

He pretended not to hear me again. As he looked at his dog, I stood my ground and said, "Are you furious because Aristotle taught you to think?"

When he pretended not to hear me, I got even angrier and shouted, "Why a human name when there are so many dog names?"

I violently squeezed the cup in my palm, breaking it in the process. I couldn't understand if it was the warm coffee from my broken cup or his blood that splashed on my clothes. I wasn't in a position to understand anyway.

I woke up with my hand warming up like that, I said to myself, "I must've had a nightmare." But what was the bloodstain on my hot pillow?

I shouldn't even think about this anymore. It was all a nightmare. The truth is, they'll be here soon. It'll just be the three of us for dinner, the two of them and myself. They should see that everything is in its place when they arrive, so they won't be suspicious. Everything has to be the same as before so they don't suspect anything. They should bring the food in from the kitchen themselves. I'll just set the table before they arrive. Let me spread the white tablecloth first. A bottle of red in the middle of the white tablecloth, a white napkin next to the bottle, and three slices of toast next to the napkin with a double-edged stiletto-like knife on the napkin with the bread. But blood should drip from the sharp end of the knife. No, they'll suspect something if they see the blood. I must do everything without arousing their suspicion. I don't care if they notice anything amiss, but all my plans will be for naught if they get carried away like before. Besides, I've had it up to here with their getting carried away for no reason, not to mention sitting under that bloody light.

www.ingramcontent.com/pod-product-compliance
Lightning Source LLC
LaVergne TN
LVHW032009070526
838202LV00059B/6367